Classic Fairy-tale Collection

Published by Top That! Publishing plc
Tide Mill Way, Woodbridge, Suffolk, IP12 1AP, UK
www.topthatpublishing.com

Published by Top That! Publishing plc
Tide Mill Way, Woodbridge, Suffolk, IP12 1AP, UK
www.topthatpublishing.com

Book illustrations by Ian Pointer
Cover illustrations by Bob Hersey

0 2 4 6 8 9 7 5 3 1
Printed and bound in China

Creative Director – Simon Couchman
Editorial Director – Daniel Graham

ISBN 978-1-78244-159-5

A catalogue record for this book is available from the British Library
Printed and bound in China

Contents

Foreword

Once upon a time, when dragons still roamed the land, people sat around their fires in the evening and told each other tales. They spoke of fearless princes, graceful princesses, wicked witches and secret hoards of treasure – every tale packed with mystery and adventure.

Over time, these tales spread throughout the world. Firstly, from village to village, then from country to country, over miles of hot desert and across deep blue oceans… and every time a tale was told it changed a little. Sometimes new characters were added, sometimes the hero was sent on an even more dangerous mission, and sometimes the storyteller decided to include some of his own country's history and traditions. Yet, no matter how much it was embellished, the basic story usually remained the same.

Told by adults to their children, and retold to their children's children, these stories were eventually collected together from all over the world. They were written down so that they could be kept safe to be enjoyed for hundreds of years to come.

Each of the sixteen fairy tales in this book is both magical and enchanting, so curl up in a favourite armchair and share these stories just as our ancestors would have done before.

Sleeping Beauty

Long ago, in a land far away, there was a castle on a hill.

In the castle lived a king and queen who were as happy as it is possible to be – except for one thing; they had no children. Day after day the queen sighed and said to herself, "How I wish I had a child."

One day the queen was sitting in her bath when a frog crawled out of the water and croaked to her, "You will have your wish. Within a year, you will give birth to a dear little girl."

When the frog's prediction came true, the queen was overjoyed. The king's eyes filled with tears of happiness as he gazed at his baby daughter. She was so beautiful and so special to him that he decided to throw a great feast to celebrate her birth. The queen agreed.

"Our daughter is a magic child," she said. "We must invite all the fairies of the kingdom to bless her and wish her well."

The king drew up a list of all their friends and relations and, as guests of honour, he invited twelve fairies. When the queen saw the list she protested, "Remember, there are thirteen fairies in the kingdom. We can't leave one out."

The king reasoned, "We have only twelve gold plates for our special guests."

"We can easily have an extra one made," replied the queen. The king put his hand on his wife's arm and whispered, "The truth is, my dear, that the thirteenth fairy is a bad fairy, who will wish nothing but trouble for our daughter. It is best she doesn't come."

So the invitations went out, and when the day came the castle was full of light and music, crackling fires and the scent of a thousand flowers. Servants rushed from the kitchen to the banqueting hall with platters of steaming food. The guests in their finery crowded around the crib to see the baby princess, toast her health and congratulate her parents on such a beautiful daughter.

As the clock struck twelve a hush descended on the happy gathering. Suddenly the air streamed with tiny sparkling stars that came from nowhere and whirled ever faster. The candle flames flickered, the curtains, the tablecloths and the ladies' skirts billowed. As the stream of stars rose, twinkling to the rafters, twelve fairies appeared. Each wore a gown of gossamer and carried a magic gift for the princess that glowed with coloured light.

One had brought the gift of carefree laughter, the next the gift of eternal sweetness, the third brought the gift of singing like a bird. Each of the fairies took their turn to lay a gift by the crib of the baby princess.

The twelfth fairy was just about to present her gift when an icy wind howled through the castle and in a puff of foul-smelling smoke a haggard figure appeared. "Why was I not invited to the party?" spat the bad fairy, her eyes flashing fire. The guests recoiled in horror and the queen ran to the crib to be near her baby.

Then the king stepped forward. "Madam, we beg your forgiveness," he began, but the bad fairy swept past him. "There are thirteen fairies in this kingdom," she rasped, "and each one of us has a gift to bring." Then she pointed a crooked finger at the baby and cried out in a loud voice, "This is my gift. When this child is sixteen years old, she will prick her finger on the spindle of a spinning wheel and drop down dead." With that she cackled an evil laugh, a choking cloud of smoke enveloped her and she disappeared.

The king and queen were distraught. They had forgotten the twelfth fairy, who had not yet given her gift. As she stepped forward, hope leaped in their hearts.

"The bad fairy is the most powerful of all the fairies," she said softly. "I cannot undo her spell. However, do not despair – luckily, my gift is the gift of sweet dreaming. With this gift I can soften the bad fairy's curse. The princess will still prick her finger on the spindle of a spinning wheel when she is sixteen years old, but she won't die. Instead, she will fall into a deep sleep, and everyone inside the castle will also fall asleep. You will all sleep for a hundred years, until the princess is woken with a kiss. That is the best I can do."

So she laid her gift by the cradle and, with that, all the fairies collected into a stream of stardust and disappeared.

The guests were left shocked and bemused. The queen hugged her daughter close. "A sleep of a hundred years!" she wept. "That is no future for our darling daughter."

"I won't let it happen," said the king firmly. "Every spinning wheel in the kingdom must be destroyed." So anyone who owned a spinning wheel brought it to the castle and threw it on a huge bonfire, singing:

"We'll burn the wicked fairy's hate
And save our princess from her fate."

Then everyone forgot about the curse. Everyone, that is, except the bad fairy.

The princess grew up to be a beautiful girl who enjoyed all the good gifts that the fairies had brought her. She was healthy and strong, could sing like a bird, and everyone loved her for her kindness and her sweet nature.

On her sixteenth birthday, the king and queen decided to hold a big party for their daughter and invite all the young princes from neighbouring kingdoms. They were sure she would fall in love with one of them and get married. They dressed her in an exquisite gown of silver and lace and gave her a necklace of rubies and moonstones to wear.

When the princess discovered their plans, she felt shy. She didn't want to get married – she wanted to stay at home with her friends. While her parents were welcoming the guests, she slipped away.

The princess skipped through the rose garden and past the stables. Suddenly she noticed a tower that she had never seen before. Its door was covered in cobwebs and there was a rusty key in the lock. Curious to find out what lay beyond, she turned the key and pushed open the door.

"Is anyone home?" she called. There was no answer, but a strange creaking sound made her take the stairs to investigate.

At the top of the tower was a tiny room. A large four-poster bed filled most of the room and right beside the bed was an old woman working at a spinning wheel. "What are you doing – and what's that?" asked the princess. (Of course, she had never seen a spinning wheel before.) The old woman replied, "I am spinning, my dear. Would you like to try it for yourself?" "Yes, please!" cried the princess excitedly. She sat down at the spinning wheel and the old woman guided her hand.

Straight away, the bad fairy's curse took effect and the princess pricked her finger on the spindle. The pain was so intense as the drops of ruby blood appeared that the princess felt cut to the heart. She collapsed onto the bed and fell into a deep, deep sleep. The bad fairy (for it was indeed her!) cackled to herself and disappeared in a puff of foul-smelling smoke.

Back in the castle, the clock in the great hall stopped ticking. The king and queen, who were sitting on their thrones welcoming their daughter's suitors, crumpled into a heap and slept.

The musicians dropped their instruments to the floor and sprawled down after them. In the kitchen, the cook slumped into the mixing bowl and the kitchen maid fell to the floor. The eggs that she carried smashed in a mess and the kitchen maid began to snore.

The stable lad collapsed into the muck heap, the horses snoozed in the straw and the dog lay down beside the cat. The pigeons on the roof stopped cooing and put their heads under their wings, the flies clung motionless to the wall and the flames in the fire died down and went out. Even the wind stopped blowing. Soon everyone in the castle was fast asleep.

As the days turned to weeks and the weeks turned to months, the castle sank deeper into its slumber. Meanwhile, briars and brambles grew all around it. Their long thorny branches straggled upwards and inwards until, after several years, the castle was completely covered. The people who lived nearby talked to their neighbours about the sleeping castle and soon the beautiful princess inside it was famous all over the world for the spell cast upon her. People called her Princess Briar Rose after the roses that bloomed every year in the thicket of thorny bushes that surrounded her home.

Over the years, many brave knights and bold princes came from every corner of the world to rescue Briar Rose and claim her hand in marriage, but each one of them failed, torn to shreds in the thorny tangle.

Then, after many, many years had passed, another young prince came to that part of the world, riding on a magnificent white horse. When he got to the thicket he was puzzled as to what lay beyond. He asked an old man who was passing by.

"My grandfather told me," said the old man, "that beyond the briars lies a castle, and behind the castle is a tower, and in the tower is a bed. On the bed lies a beautiful princess, cursed to sleep for a hundred years."

The young prince vowed to go to the princess and break the curse. The old man shook his head and tried to dissuade him, telling of all the others before him who had failed and died.

The prince, however, was determined. As he approached the thicket all the briars and the brambles parted to let the prince through, and closed again behind him. It was a hundred years since the princess had fallen asleep… the time had come for her rescue.

Inside the thorny hedge the prince saw a garden with a gardener lying asleep by his barrow. Beyond the garden were the stables where the stable boy lay in the muck heap and the horses snoozed on the straw. At the door of the castle the prince saw the king and queen, collapsed in all their finery, and inside, the musicians snored by their instruments. In the kitchen, the prince came across the cook and the kitchen maid fast asleep. Even the birds, the mice and the flies slept. The whole place was so quiet that the prince could hear himself breathe.

At the back of the stables the prince found the tower. The rusty key still turned so he pushed open the creaky door and climbed the stairs. At the top of the stairs was a small room with a big bed. On the bed lay a beautiful princess, asleep in a dress of silver and lace with a string of rubies and moonstones around her neck. The prince gazed in wonder at the girl. She was so beautiful that tears came to his eyes. How can she have been asleep for a hundred years, he thought, she looks as though she lay down to rest just a moment ago. Without thinking about what he was doing, the prince bent over the girl. His hand brushed her hair from her face and, very tenderly, his lips met hers in a kiss.

Princess Briar Rose sighed and her eyelids fluttered. Then she stretched and yawned and opened her eyes from the sweetest dream.

"Who are you?" she asked.

In the kitchen, the cook lifted her head from the mixing bowl and the kitchen girl picked herself up from the floor. All over the castle things sprang

back to life. The pigeons on the roof cooed, the flies started buzzing, the horses neighed and the stable boy picked himself up off the muck heap. The cat and dog began to fight, the clock ticked, the wind blew and the flames flickered around the logs in the hearth.

In the tower, the prince knelt before Princess Briar Rose. "You are so beautiful, I can hardly believe you are over a hundred years old," he murmured. Briar Rose laughed. "What do you mean?" she asked. "Today is my sixteenth birthday!" "Will you marry me?" asked the prince. To her surprise, Briar Rose was so overcome with love for the handsome young man that she agreed. They were married that very same day and what started as a birthday feast became a wedding party!

THE END

Rapunzel

Once upon a time, a man and his wife lived in a cottage that looked out onto a beautiful garden. The couple couldn't go into the garden, however, because it belonged to a wicked witch.

One day, the wife spotted a bright green plant she had never seen before.

"What is that strange plant growing in the witch's garden?" she asked her husband.

"It's called rapunzel," he replied.

The woman felt a sudden craving. "I must have some rapunzel to eat or I will surely die."

Her husband was taken aback. "You know I can't go into the witch's garden and steal her plants," he said.

Although the very thought of entering the garden filled him with dread, he loved his wife dearly and didn't like to see her so upset. When night fell, he climbed out of the window and picked a bunch of rapunzel from the garden.

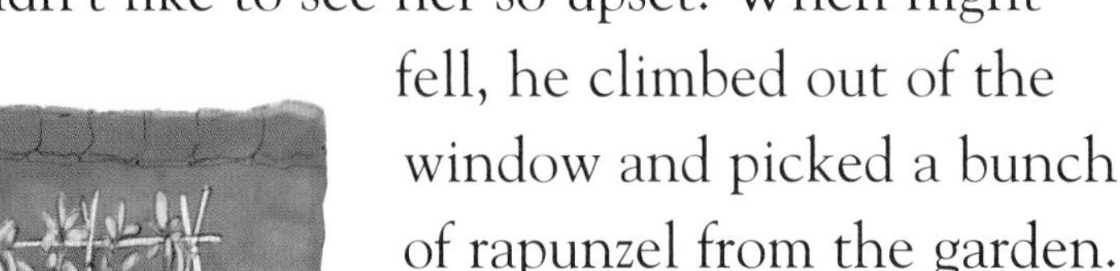

When he got back indoors, his wife snatched the rapunzel from him and made the bright green leaves into a wonderful salad.

The next night the same thing happened. The wife pleaded with her husband to fetch more rapunzel, so, once again, he entered the witch's garden. This time, however, someone was waiting for him.

"What are you doing in my garden?" said a sharp, cracked voice.

The man gasped. "My wife is ill and she must have rapunzel to eat," he explained. The witch (for indeed it was her) looked at him with her menacing black eyes.

"Your wife is not ill," she said. "She is expecting a baby and if she craves rapunzel to eat, she must have it. Pick as much as you want."

The man was overjoyed, but then the witch added darkly, "However, when the child is born, you must give it to me," and with that, she vanished.

The man hardly knew what to think. He was happy and scared all at once. He picked a big bunch of rapunzel and hurried home.

In due course, the wife gave birth to a baby girl. "Rapunzel," she murmured, "we must call her Rapunzel."

When the baby was only a few days old, the haggard old witch appeared at the door, just as she said she would. "I have come for your daughter," she cackled. Then she snatched the baby and disappeared!

Rapunzel grew up to be an exceptionally beautiful girl with long, golden hair. Worried that someone would steal Rapunzel from her, the witch took her deep into the forest and locked her up in a tall, round tower. The doorway was blocked off and the staircase knocked down to make sure no one could get in or out.

The witch visited Rapunzel every day to bring her food and to brush her long hair. As there was no way into the tower she called out:

> "Rapunzel, Rapunzel,
> Let down your hair!"

Rapunzel then dropped her golden locks from the window for the witch to twist into a rope to climb up.

In between the witch's visits there was nothing for Rapunzel to do but sing. She had the sweetest voice and when she sang, the birds sang with her.

One beautiful spring day, a noble young prince was riding through the forest. Lost in his thoughts, he suddenly realised the air was full of song. He followed the sweet sound until he came to the mysterious tower.

Suddenly the singing stopped and a chill descended on the forest. The prince hid himself and watched to see what would happen.

A ragged old witch emerged into the clearing and called up to the tower:

"Rapunzel, Rapunzel,
Let down your hair!"

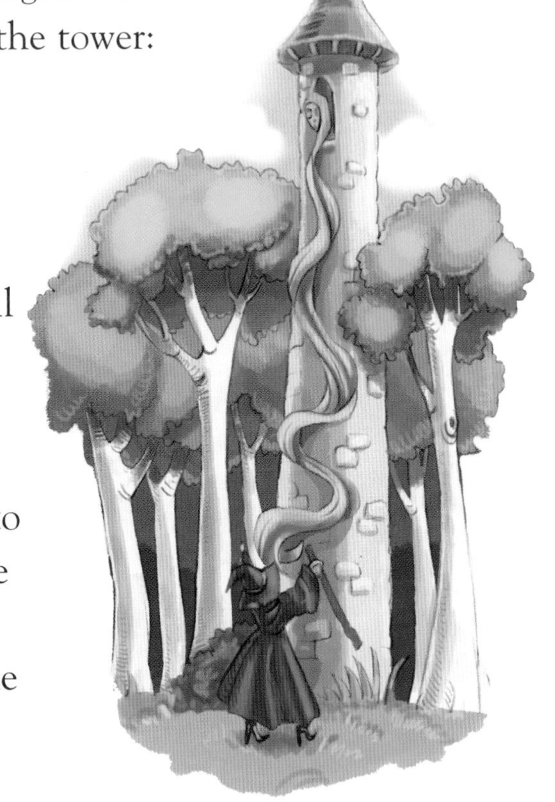

A long, sparkling waterfall of golden hair came tumbling down. The witch hitched up her skirts, twisted the hair into a rope and climbed up the tower. After a while, the prince saw the witch come back down again and disappear into the forest.

The prince was curious to find out who had such wonderful hair and such a sweet singing voice. He waited until he was sure the witch had gone, then called out:

"Rapunzel, Rapunzel,
Let down your hair!"

The waterfall of hair came tumbling down, glinting in the sunlight. The prince took the soft, sweet-smelling hair in his hands, twisted it gently into a rope and began to climb. When he reached the top and saw the lovely face of Rapunzel his heart beat very fast and he was overcome with love. As for Rapunzel, she was so surprised to see this handsome young man that she almost fainted.

The prince clasped her in his arms, their lips touched and, for the first time in her life, Rapunzel knew true happiness.

"I will love you for ever," the prince promised Rapunzel, "and I would like you to be my wife." Rapunzel nodded and her eyes filled with tears of joy.

Together they planned Rapunzel's escape. They decided that the prince would visit Rapunzel every day, bringing a skein of silk each time which Rapunzel could make into a ladder. Then the prince would be able to climb up and rescue her from the tower. Sure enough, the prince arrived at the tower every day with a skein of silk and Rapunzel began to weave the ladder in the hope of her escape.

The day finally came when the ladder was ready. As the witch made her morning visit, Rapunzel rubbed her head. “You are so much heavier than…” She stopped, aghast, but the damage had been done.

“Heavier than who?” snapped the witch.

Rapunzel cast her eyes to the floor. “Heavier than the prince,” she whispered.

The witch was furious. “Wicked child!” she screamed. Quick as a flash, she took out a huge pair of scissors from under her robe and snipped off Rapunzel’s beautiful hair. Then she made Rapunzel climb down the silk ladder to wander the forest alone.

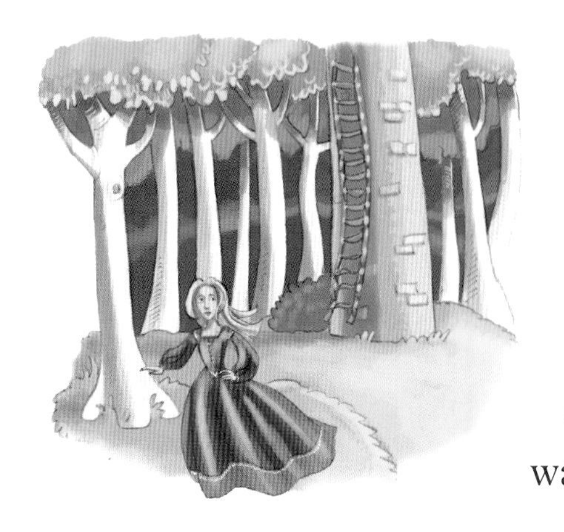

That evening, the prince stood at the bottom of the tower and called out for what he hoped would be the last time:

"Rapunzel, Rapunzel,
Let down your hair!"

To his delight, Rapunzel's silken ladder came tumbling down. He quickly climbed to the top, and was horrified when he found himself face to face with the haggard old witch! "Rapunzel has gone," the witch cackled with glee and, with a snip of her scissors, she cut the silken ladder from the window and sent the prince tumbling to the ground.

His fall was broken by a bush of thorns which pricked his eyes and blinded him. The prince stumbled into the forest, his whole world plunged into darkness.

For many months, the prince and Rapunzel wandered alone on different paths. Their only friends were the birds who sang to them, reminding them of the first time they met.

After a year and a day, Rapunzel came across the prince asleep under a tree. She ran joyfully to him and embraced him. As her tears bathed his face, they fell into his eyes and made him see again.

Overjoyed, the prince took Rapunzel to his palace where they were soon married. Rapunzel was reunited with her parents and everyone was happy. The witch couldn't get down from the tower because it had no door and no staircase. She was stuck up there for a very long time!

THE END

The Ugly Duckling

Deep in the heart of the countryside lay a farm where a mother duck sat patiently minding her eggs. One day, having returned from a walk to stretch her legs, she noticed there were seven eggs in her nest instead of six. "That's very strange," she murmured to herself, "I don't remember laying such a large egg."

A little later, one of the farmyard hens came strutting across. "Not done yet, then?" she enquired (for hens like to keep up with the farmyard gossip).

"No," replied the duck with a sigh as she shifted herself into a more comfortable position.

Suddenly there was a 'crack'... 'crack, crack'. The eggs had started hatching! Six cute and fluffy yellow ducklings soon looked up at their mother who quacked proudly beside her new family.

However, one egg – the largest one – had not yet hatched. "Oh bother," muttered the duck as she sat back down on the nest, "I wonder how much longer I shall have to sit here."

The ducklings played around the nest, exploring their new world, while their mother waited patiently. It wasn't long before another 'crack' was heard. Jumping up, the mother duck stood ready to welcome the last little yellow duckling to her brood. To everyone's surprise, however, a large, grey, scruffy duckling popped out of the egg!

The next day, the whole brood went to the pond for their first swimming lesson. As they waddled through the farmyard, the other animals stood and stared. Following the mother duck were six fluffy, yellow ducklings and one large, scruffy, grey duckling. The animals didn't know what to make of it. The hen eventually said what all the other animals were thinking. "Look at that scruffy, grey duckling," she clucked, "she's so ugly!"

With that, the other duckling's roared with laughter. "Ugly duckling, ugly duckling," they chanted together.

"Don't be so unkind," scolded the mother duck, and hurried her family on towards the pond.

The six little ducklings jumped into the water, quacking excitedly, but the ugly duckling, embarrassed and ashamed, hid herself in some reeds near by.

A little while later, the ugly duckling came out from the reeds and slipped into the water. She discovered she could swim quite easily and started to feel much happier.

Near by, a toad sat on a lily pad, watching the new family. As the ugly duckling swam past, trying to catch up with her brothers and sisters, it shouted out, "Goodness, gracious me – you're an ugly duckling!"

The mother duck was furious. "Leave her alone," she quacked, "it's not her fault."

The poor little duckling felt unloved and unwanted. She felt so sad and lonely, she decided to run away.

That night, as the other ducklings slept soundly, the ugly duckling left the farm. On her way, she passed the pig sty. A large, muddy pig poked its large snout through the fence and snorted, “My goodness, you’re an ugly duckling.” The duckling, who had grown used to the insults by now, looked up at the mud-covered pig and replied, “You don’t look too good yourself!”

Getting tired, the ugly duckling began to look for a place to rest. She could see an old barn ahead with one of its wide doors slightly ajar. She crept inside, being careful not to disturb the sleeping cows, and made herself comfortable on a bed of hay. In no time at all she was sound asleep.

When morning came, the loud mooing of the cows woke her. The oldest and wisest of the cows came over to introduce herself to this stranger in the barn. The little duckling looked up into its large brown eyes and began to explain why she had run away from home.

The cow felt sorry for the ugly duckling and suggested that maybe she should go to the forest. She had heard there were many different creatures living there and supposed that some might be ugly too. The duckling thanked the wise cow for her advice and headed off towards the forest.

Just as she was beginning to feel very hungry, the ugly duckling spotted a large scarecrow in the middle of a field. Scattered around it were pieces of bread, probably dropped by the crows it had scared away. Wasting no time, the duckling gobbled up the bread.

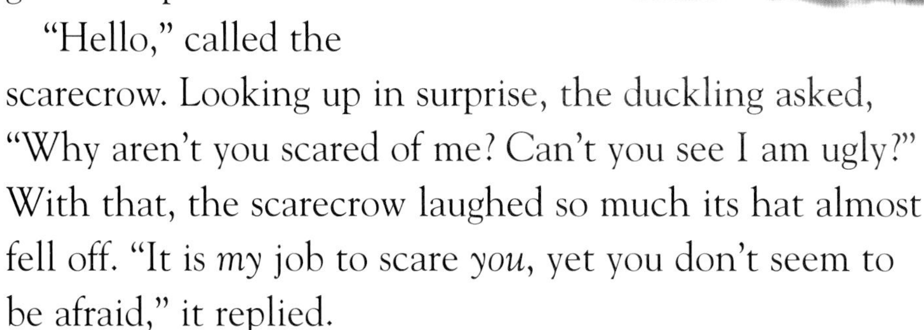

"Hello," called the scarecrow. Looking up in surprise, the duckling asked, "Why aren't you scared of me? Can't you see I am ugly?" With that, the scarecrow laughed so much its hat almost fell off. "It is *my* job to scare *you*, yet you don't seem to be afraid," it replied.

The duckling told her sad tale while the scarecrow listened with interest. On finishing her story, the ugly duckling felt much better. It had been nice chatting to the scarecrow and she called a cheery 'goodbye' as she set off once more for the forest.

It was late by the time the duckling reached the edge of the forest. Huge trees towered above her and the undergrowth appeared tangled and menacing. Not knowing where to turn, the little duckling crouched in a hollow at the base of a giant oak tree. Afraid to close her eyes, she sat listening to the strange sounds around her as the sky grew darker and night fell.

The duckling tried to get some sleep, but as the night-time creatures came out from their hiding places, she sat and watched them in wonder. Maybe the reason the badgers and hedgehogs came out at night was because, like her, they were afraid of being seen. She longed to join in their fun and games.

The duckling had been in the forest for some time when, early one bright morning, she sensed a change in the air. The animals that usually ran about the forest were strangely quiet and didn't come out from their hiding places. Suddenly, the peace of the forest was shattered by loud bangs, and blue smoke drifted high above the trees.

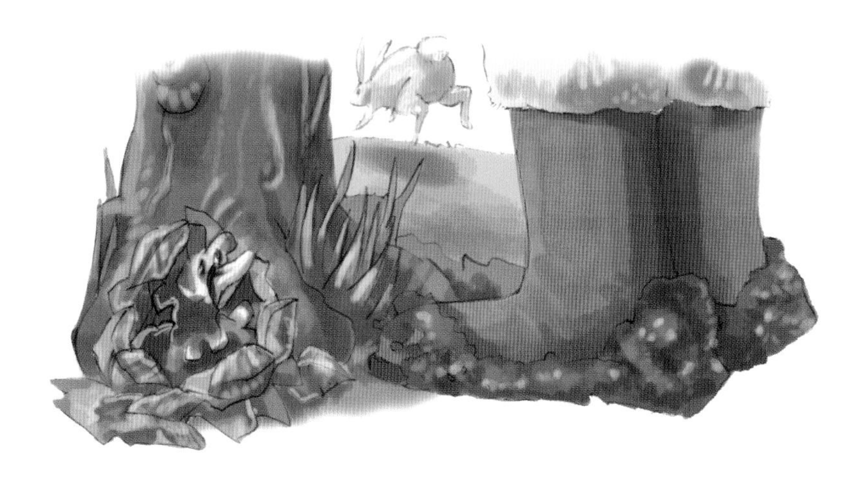

Terrified, the duckling stayed hidden in the hollow at the base of the giant oak tree. A fierce-looking dog came bounding up to her and started sniffing around. The duckling froze with fear, scared that the dog would grab her with its sharp teeth. One of the men had a gun slung over his shoulder. He shouted to the dog which ran off, leaving the trembling duckling alone.

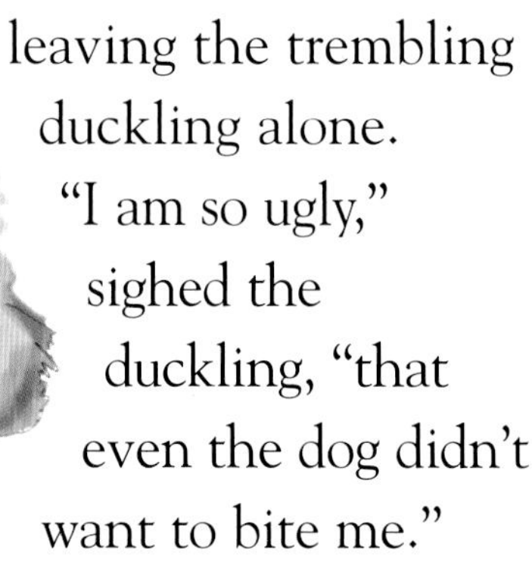

"I am so ugly," sighed the duckling, "that even the dog didn't want to bite me."

It was some time before peace was restored to the forest. The animals cautiously came out from their hiding places, but the ugly duckling didn't feel safe any longer. Once again, she set off into the unknown. As she walked, a flock of swans flew overhead. They had long, graceful necks and their gleaming white feathers shone in the winter sun. The ugly duckling gazed up at them in awe.

With the forest far behind her, the duckling sat down to rest. A little while later, an old woman came puffing up the hill on her way home from the village. She sat herself down on the stump of a tree and, taking a look around her, spotted the duckling. "Oh, you poor little thing!" she exclaimed. "You will never survive the winter out here. Let me take you home to my warm cottage." With that, she scooped up the duckling and put it in her basket.

Paint was peeling from the old woman's cottage, the gate hung on one hinge and the garden was overgrown with weeds, but it looked safe and cosy to the trembling duckling.

As they entered the cottage, a large black cat opened a sleepy eye from where it was curled up on a battered armchair. "We have a visitor, Velvet," said the old woman as she bent down to stroke the cat's soft fur. She put the ugly duckling down on the rug in front of the fire and went to her tiny kitchen to make some tea.

The black cat looked down at the duckling, her yellow eyes glinting. "You ugly little duckling," she hissed. "How dare you come in to my home and steal my mistress's affections."

As time passed, the ugly duckling became more and more unhappy. Although the old woman was kindness itself, the spiteful cat found a new way to tease and taunt the little duckling every day.

One evening, while the old woman slept in her rocking chair by the fire, Velvet crept up behind the duckling. "I think it is about time you left this house," she hissed, and lashed out at the duckling with her sharp claws.

Luckily, the old woman woke from her sleep in time to stop any real harm being done, but it was no good... the duckling could bear it no longer.

Early the next morning, despite the snow that covered everything in a thick, white layer, the duckling left the warmth of the cottage. She gave one last look behind her and saw a trail of little footprints in the newly fallen snow. Then she noticed Velvet watching her from the windowsill. As the cat sat licking her paws and preening herself, the duckling pressed on, determined to leave the jealous creature far behind.

The ugly duckling passed a field where a snowman stood. Birds were pecking at the carrot that was its nose and the duckling wondered if the snowman felt as miserable as she did.

Eventually, she reached the edge of the riverbank and, looking around for a place to hide, found a large clump of weeds close to the water. "No-one will catch sight of me here," she sighed. It was a very lonely time for the little duckling.

As winter turned to spring, the snow melted away and daffodils lifted their heads to the warmth of the sun. The ugly duckling watched from her lonely hideout as families with young children came to the riverbank to feed the ducks. How she longed to join in. Instead, when no one was looking, she would come out of hiding to eat the leftover bread.

One day, a group of swans glided by. "They are such graceful creatures," murmured the duckling to herself. Fascinated, she crept out from her hiding place, hoping to get a closer look. Leaning through the reeds, she suddenly caught sight of a beautiful swan staring straight at her! Horrified at what this elegant creature might think, she quickly stuck her head in the water to hide her face.

A young boy, holding his mother's hand and clutching a bag of bread, shouted out, "Look, a baby swan!" Jumping up and down with excitement, the little boy threw a handful of bread into the water.

The group of swans came swimming back towards the waiting food. The duckling froze… she had no time to hide. The swans circled around her and stroked her with their beaks. “You are such a beautiful, young swan,” they said. Astounded, she took a look at her reflection in the water. “I really am a swan!” she cried out joyfully. With her head held high, she proudly flapped her wings and joined the other swans.

All the hardships she had been through hardly seemed to matter now. She had such joy in her heart, for she knew that when others stared at her, it was because she was a beautiful swan. Never again would she be called an ugly duckling!

THE END

Beauty and the Beast

Once upon a time there was a very rich merchant who had three daughters – Stella, Della and Bella. They were all beautiful girls, but the youngest, Bella, had a kind heart and was always cheerful. In fact, she was so lovely that everyone called her Beauty.

The merchant gave his daughters everything they could wish for, but their luck was soon to change. One terrible day, disaster struck and the merchant lost all his money.

"This is too bad," shrieked Stella. "How am I to buy a new dress for the ball?"

"It's not fair," shouted Della, stamping her foot, "you promised me a new gold necklace."

"I'm sorry, my dears," said the merchant wearily, "but without money we won't be able to buy anything – not even bread."

Beauty ran to her father to comfort him. "Don't worry, papa," she cried. "We can sell our silver to buy flour and I will make our bread."

The merchant smiled, but he knew he had to earn money to keep the family together.

"I'll set off straight away to the north to meet new traders and make our fortune again," he vowed.

"Don't come back without bringing us presents!" cried Stella and Della, jumping up and down with glee. "A new dress and a golden necklace, remember?"

"What shall I bring back for my youngest daughter?" the merchant asked Beauty tenderly.

"Bring me a rose, papa," she whispered, kissing him on the cheek.

The merchant mounted his horse and set off on his journey. He was so troubled by his misfortune, however, that he strayed from the path and by nightfall was lost deep in the forest.

The merchant's horse wearily ambled on until, suddenly, its hoof struck something that glinted in the moonlight. The merchant dismounted to take a closer look and realised that he was peering into a mirror. In the mirror he saw a castle, lost in the forest just as he was.

As he stared at the castle a chill ran through his body and mist swirled before his eyes. Something very strange was happening!

When the mist had cleared, the merchant looked around in astonishment – he was standing inside the very same castle he had seen in the mirror! A long table lay before him with a place set for one. The merchant saw steaming bowls of carrots and potatoes, a dish full of oranges and nuts and a roast chicken on a platter, its skin crisp and golden. Although he was hungry after his long journey, he did not dare sit down to eat.

"Is anyone home?" called the merchant. The echoes of his voice faded to silence... there was no reply. As the merchant wandered through the vast halls of the mysterious castle, he soon came to realise that the statues lining the corridors wore blindfolds and the mirrors that hung on the walls were cracked.

Having seen no signs of life, the merchant returned to the dining hall where he sat down and ate a good dinner. Then, feeling extremely tired, he fell into a deep sleep.

In the morning the merchant ate the breakfast he found waiting for him, then wandered out into the garden. It was full of roses. His eyes misted with tears as he thought of his daughter, Beauty. "I will pick you a rose, my beauty," he whispered, and selected a ruby red rose with the morning dew still shimmering on its petals.

As the merchant picked the rose a shadow fell over him and he turned to face the most hideous creature he had ever seen.

"How dare you steal from me," growled the Beast. "For this you must die!"

The merchant fell to his knees. "Spare me, Beast," he gasped. "Spare me for the sake of my daughters. They will be orphans if I die." A tear rolled down his cheek and fell twinkling onto the ruby red rose. "I plucked this rose for my youngest daughter, Beauty, the sweetest girl in the world. I meant no harm."

The Beast's ears perked up and he snorted with interest. "I will spare you on one condition," he said, cocking his head thoughtfully. "You may live, but you must send me your daughter in your place. Here is a bag of gold to help you on your way."

Before the merchant could protest that he would rather die than part with Beauty, a mist descended upon him, he felt weak and dizzy, then everything went dark.

The merchant woke to find himself sitting on his horse in the forest. His horse set off calmly towards home just as if nothing had happened. Only the bag of gold in his hand convinced the merchant that he hadn't been dreaming.

Eventually the merchant reached the gate of his house and his daughters rushed out to welcome him.

"Papa," cried Della, taking the bag from him, "you have already been lucky in business!"

"Here's enough gold for new dresses for all of us as well as gold necklaces studded with gems," laughed Stella.

"I am so happy to see you, my dearest papa," smiled Beauty as her father handed her the rose.

That evening, the merchant told his daughters what had happened to him at the Beast's castle and, with a heavy heart, repeated the promise he had made to the hideous creature.

"Forget your promise," snarled Stella. "We have the gold and that is all that matters."

Beauty put down her knife and fork and said quietly, "I am not afraid of the Beast. We must honour your promise, papa, then nothing bad will happen to any of us. I will go to the castle."

The following morning, a white horse with plumes on its head was waiting outside the merchant's house. Still clutching her rose, Beauty mounted the horse and promised her father she would return as soon as she was able. The horse turned and set off for the forest.

Hours later, the horse just stopped. Beauty looked down and realised that the mirror her father had told her about was at the horse's feet. As she stared into the glass, a chill ran through her body and mist swirled in front of her eyes. When the mist cleared, Beauty found herself standing inside the great hall of the Beast's castle.

It was just as her father had described. She sat down at the table set for one and ate dinner, then she lay down in a luxurious feather bed and slept. In the morning she wandered in the rose garden and thought of home. Beauty was troubled at the thought of meeting with the ugly creature her father had described, but, in a voice that sounded braver than she felt, she called out to the Beast. Silence... no one came.

For days Beauty lived alone. The only signs that the Beast was nearby were the delicious meals that appeared every day and the presents that she found at the end of her bed when she woke each morning.

Beauty grew so lonely that she longed for company, even that of the Beast. One night, she hid in the darkness at the bottom of the stairs and touched his hairy hand as he passed. Just at that moment the Moon appeared from behind a cloud and lit up his face. Beauty gasped in horror. The Beast was so dreadfully ugly that she thought she would die.

A tear rolled down the Beast's warty face as he watched Beauty recoil in fright. "I must be the ugliest thing you have ever seen," he said sadly.

Beauty swallowed her fear and answered, "Sir, I cannot judge, for I have seen very little of the world."

So the Beast gave Beauty a magic mirror in which she could see what the world was like.

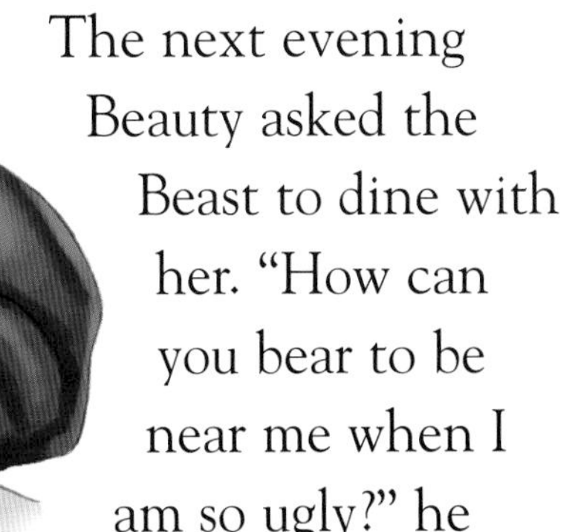

The next evening Beauty asked the Beast to dine with her. "How can you bear to be near me when I am so ugly?" he said, hanging his head in shame.

"Indeed you are not," said Beauty. "I saw war and famine in the mirror, and violence and cruelty. Those are the ugliest things I have ever seen." The Beast looked down at her and smiled.

After that, he and Beauty spent all their time talking and laughing together and walking in the rose garden.

One day, Beauty asked the Beast if she could go home to visit her family as she could see in the mirror that her father was missing her terribly. The Beast rolled his eyes in fear. "Never!" he snorted. "You must never leave me for I fear you will not return."

Beauty gently reminded him that she had kept her father's promise and that she would definitely come back.

Reluctantly, the Beast let Beauty go as long as she took the magic mirror with her so that she could see him whenever she wanted.

Beauty set off early the next morning. As she turned to wave to the Beast, the sky darkened over the castle and brambles seemed to spring up before her very eyes. Although sad to leave the Beast, Beauty was anxious to be reunited with her father.

When she reached home at last, Beauty's father rushed out to greet her with tears in his eyes, closely followed by Stella and Della who wanted to know what the commotion was about.

"The house has become a terrible mess without you," shrieked Stella.

"That's right," screeched Della. "There's a pile of ironing to do and we haven't eaten properly for months."

Beauty simply smiled. She was so pleased to be home with her family that she set to with a will, cleaning and cooking until the house felt like home again and the larder was full. While Beauty swept and baked, her sisters chattered happily about parties and fancy clothes, and the weeks sped by.

One night, Beauty remembered the mirror which lay hidden beneath her pillow. She suddenly felt very anxious about the Beast who had been so kind to her. Peering into the mirror she saw the most terrible sight.

The roses in the Beast's garden were dying, and lying beneath the fallen petals was a dark shape. With a shock, Beauty realised it was the Beast and that he was barely breathing.

"My poor Beast!" she cried, leaping up. "Why have I neglected you?" She ran to the beautiful white horse that was already pawing the ground, then set off at a gallop until she reached the castle.

Beauty pushed her way through thorny twigs and creepers. Her dress was torn and her hands were bleeding when she finally reached the rose garden. "Oh, my dear Beast," she sobbed, taking his poor head in her hands, "forgive me for breaking my promise. Please don't die, Beast – I love you."

At those words, the Beast opened his eyes and something miraculous occurred. His ugliness began to fade away: his lumpy flesh became slender and muscular, his warty, hairy skin turned smooth and his eyes grew lustrous and shining. The Beast was transformed into a handsome young man.

"Who are you?" gasped Beauty in amazement. "Where is the Beast that I love?"

"I have not changed inside," said the young man softly. "Long ago I used to be a prince and I looked as I do right now, but a spell was cast upon me, cursing me with the ugliness of the Beast. That spell was to have power over me until someone declared they loved me for myself and not for my looks. Now, dear Beauty, you have told me that you love me and the curse has been lifted."

As they gazed in rapture at one another a second miracle happened. The dead rose garden burst into life. The brambles smothering the lonely castle disappeared and the air was filled with birdsong.

The handsome prince and the beautiful girl sealed their love with a kiss, promising to be faithful to one another for ever.

THE END

The Three Little Pigs

Once upon a time there were three little pigs who lived comfortably at home with their mother. However, the day came when they were not quite so little – in fact, they had grown so much that there was no longer enough room for them in their mother's house.

"Although we have all been very happy here," said the mother pig, "it's time you built houses of your own, my dears. There's a big, wide world out there waiting to be explored. Now, let your wise old mother give you an important piece of advice." She cleared her throat. "My dears," she said, "whatever you do in life, make sure you do it to the very best of your ability." The little pigs snuffled politely and nudged one another. They were eager to set out on their journey.

The next morning, their mother saw them on their way. She gave each little pig a piece of bread and an orange tied in a red-spotted handkerchief which they carried on sticks over their shoulders.

Further down the road, the three little pigs met a man with a cart loaded with straw. "Look at that!" cried the first little pig. "Ideal building material!"

He asked the man whether he could have some straw with which to build a house. The man agreed and in no time at all the little pig had built himself a fine house of straw. He was very proud of his new house, but the other little pigs walked on. They remembered the words of their wise old mother. "We can do better than that," they whispered to each other.

A little bit further along the road, the two little pigs met a man with a cart loaded with sticks. "Now, look at that!" exclaimed the second little pig. "That's what I call ideal building material!"

He asked the man whether he could have some sticks with which to build a house. The man agreed and in two or three days the little pig had built himself a house of sticks. He was very proud of his handsome stick house, but the other little pig walked on. He remembered the words of his wise old mother. "I can do better than that," he thought to himself.

Further along the road, the little pig met a man with a cart loaded with bricks.

"This is what I've been waiting for!" said the little pig. "Those bricks will make ideal building material!"

He asked the man if he could have some bricks with which to build a house. The man agreed and after a lot of hard work that took a very long time indeed, the little pig had built himself a solid house of bricks. He was very proud of his sturdy brick house – it would be cosy in winter and cool in summer.

Now, the mother pig used to tell her sons about a big, bad wolf that lived in the neighbouring woods. This big, bad wolf was always very hungry and his favourite food was plump, juicy piglet! One day, the wolf was strolling down the road when he spied the first little pig sunning himself in the garden in front of his house of straw.

"Hah! Little pig!" cried the wolf. "Come here so I can eat you for my dinner!" The little pig squealed and ran inside his straw house. "Little pig, little pig, let me come in!" roared the wolf. The little pig was terrified. "Oh, no! Not by the hair on my chinny chin chin!" he squeaked.

"Then I'll huff and I'll puff and I'll blow your house in!" growled the wolf. The wolf took a deep breath, then he huffed and he puffed. He blew down the house of straw and ate the little pig for his dinner!

Several days had passed and the wolf was strolling down the road when, suddenly, he spied the second little pig picking flowers in the garden outside his house of sticks.

"Hah! Little pig!" cried the wolf. "Come here so I can eat you for my dinner!" The little pig squealed and ran inside his house of sticks. "Little pig, little pig, let me come in," roared the wolf. The little pig was terrified. "Oh, no! Not by the hair on my chinny chin chin!" he squeaked.

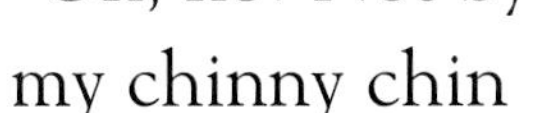

"Then I'll huff and I'll puff and I'll blow your house in!" growled the wolf. The wolf took a deep breath, then he huffed and he puffed. He blew down the house of sticks and ate the little pig for his dinner!

Several days later, the wolf's stomach began to rumble. It was time to eat again. He spied the third little pig digging in the vegetable patch outside his house of bricks.

"Hah! Little pig!" cried the wolf. "Come here so I can eat you for my dinner!" The little pig squealed and ran inside his house of bricks.

"Little pig, little pig, let me come in," roared the wolf. The little pig was terrified. "Oh, no! Not by the hair on my chinny chin chin!" he squeaked.

"Then I'll huff and I'll puff and I'll blow your house in!" growled the wolf.

The wolf took a breath so big that he thought his lungs would burst. He huffed and he puffed but, no matter how hard he tried, he could not blow down the house of bricks. This made the wolf very angry…

The next day, the wolf went to the little pig's house and called out in his most charming voice, "Hello, my friend. I'd like to show you where some nice turnips grow. Be ready tomorrow morning at six o'clock and we'll go to the field to dig them up together."

The little pig liked turnips, so he agreed. The wolf smiled a charming smile, but this little pig wasn't stupid. He knew the big, bad wolf wanted to trick him and would gobble him up with razor-sharp teeth.

The next morning, the little pig got up at five o'clock and went to the turnip field on his own. He dug up a whole basketful of big turnips and brought them home. When the wolf arrived to call for him, the little pig said, "I've already been to the field and dug up some turnips. As you can see, I'm cooking them for my dinner." The little pig pointed to the pot over his fire where the turnips were bubbling nicely.

The wolf was furious. He paced up and down outside the little pig's brick house until, suddenly, he had another idea.

Coming back to the window, he said in his most charming voice, "My friend, I'd like to show you where some sweet, crunchy apples grow. Be ready tomorrow morning at five o'clock and we'll go to the orchard to pick them together." The little pig liked apples, so he agreed. The wolf smiled a charming smile, but this little pig wasn't stupid. He knew the big, bad wolf still wanted to trick him and gobble him up for dinner.

The next morning the little pig got up at four o'clock and went to the orchard on his own. He picked a whole basket of sweet, crunchy apples and was just about to climb down from the tree when a voice called to him.

"Hah! Little pig! So you got here first!" snarled the big, bad wolf.

The little pig was so shaken that he almost dropped the basket of apples he'd collected.

He pretended he wasn't frightened at all, however, and called down to the wolf, "The apples are as sweet and crunchy as you promised. Here, try one!"

With that, the little pig threw the wolf an apple which whizzed past his ear and rolled down the road. While the wolf was running after the apple, the little pig quickly climbed down from the tree. He scampered as fast as his legs would carry him to the safety of his strong brick house.

When the wolf realised what had happened, he was really mad. He stamped around beneath the apple tree, growling and snarling until, suddenly, he had an idea. He went to the little pig's house and put his head to the window.

"My friend," said the wolf in his most charming voice, "the fair is coming to town tomorrow. I will come and fetch you at two in the afternoon and we can go there to ride the swingboats together."

The little pig agreed because there was nothing he liked better than riding swingboats at a fair. The wolf smiled his most charming smile, showing all his teeth, and sloped off.

The next day, the little pig set off early to the fair. When he arrived, he rode on the swingboats to his heart's content. Then he bought a big wooden barrel, for he had decided to press his own apple juice. The little pig was on his way home, bowling the barrel along in front of him, when he saw the big, bad wolf swaggering towards him. This terrible sight made the little pig's knees tremble… but then he had a brilliant idea.

Quick as a flash, the little pig hid inside the barrel. It rolled down the road, building up such a speed that it knocked the wolf down and rolled right over him! The wolf sat up and, rubbing the bump on the top of his head, wondered what had hit him! Meanwhile, the little pig laughed all the way back to his home.

The next day, the wolf went to the little pig's house. He put his head to the window and said, "Well, my friend, I didn't see you at the fair yesterday."

"Oh, I was there," said the little pig. I got there early. I rode on the swing boats, then I bought myself a barrel and rolled all the way home in it. In fact, I believe I rolled right over you!" He put his trotter up to his mouth and snuffled a laugh.

The big, bad wolf looked at the little pig, then he looked at the barrel, and he knew that the story was true. He was so full of rage that he thought he would burst – he didn't like being tricked by anyone. The wolf stopped pretending to smile and said in a gruff and terrible voice, "Little pig, I am going to eat you for my dinner right now!" The little pig was very frightened, but he didn't show it. "On no you won't!" he cried. "Not by the hair on my chinny chin chin!" The wolf, however, was determined.

"I'm going to climb onto your roof, then down your chimney, then I'm going to eat you up," he roared. His eyes were red as coals, he was so angry. The little pig thought quickly and, as he saw the wolf's tail disappearing above the window, he had an idea.

The little pig set his pot of water over the fire, then he blew the flames with his bellows until the fire was blazing and the water inside the pot was bubbling fiercely. Then, just as the little pig had hoped, the big, bad wolf jumped down the chimney and fell straight into the pot of boiling water… and that was the end of him!

When the little pig's mother heard this story, she was very proud of her son. He had always kept his wits about him and done everything to the very best of his ability – he was a very clever little pig indeed.

THE END

Goldilocks and the Three Bears

Once upon a long time ago, there was a little girl called Goldilocks. She was called Goldilocks because she had lovely long golden hair, which her mother usually tied up into two bunches. Sometimes she wore red ribbons in her hair, and sometimes she wore blue ones. She lived with her mummy and daddy in a beautiful house right on the edge of a very big wood.

One day, Goldilocks was fed up. She tugged the end of one of her blue ribbons. She had played all of the games that one could possibly play. "I'm ever so bored Mummy," she sighed.

Her mother, who had just finished washing the breakfast dishes, said, "Why don't you go for a walk in the woods?"

"What a good idea," said Goldilocks. So off she went, down the garden path, through the black iron gate, and in to the woods.

She wandered amongst the rustling trees. The sun was shining and the air was warm on her face. The birds whistled a merry tune and, way up above her, the squirrels darted from one branch to another. As she ventured deeper and deeper into the woods, the undergrowth became thicker and thicker.

Pushing through the bushes, Goldilocks suddenly came to a clearing. In the distance, she saw a little cottage with a thatched roof. There was a wisp of white smoke curling out of the chimney. The big, blue front door was wide open.

A lovely smell wafted towards her through the opening. Lifting her nose and taking a deep breath, she followed the smell. Stepping into the cool hallway she called out, "Hello, is there anybody at home?" There was no answer. There didn't seem to be anybody in. The only sound Goldilocks could hear was the crackling of wood burning on a fire.

Curious and now very hungry, Goldilocks wandered down the hall into the big kitchen. On the wooden table there were three bowls of porridge. They looked as though they'd just been served. One of the bowls was huge – it was the size of a large cooking pot! Another was the size of a saucepan and the other one was tiny.

Standing on a chair so that she could reach, Goldilocks pitched the spoon into the largest bowl. She scooped up a spoonful of porridge and then placed it into her mouth. "Ouch!" she squealed, and dropped the spoon.

The porridge was far too hot. It had burnt her tongue! She grabbed a glass of water and gulped it down. When her tongue had cooled off, she tried the saucepan-sized bowl of porridge. "Yuck!" she said and pulled a horrible face. It was far too cold and sticky. Then she tried the tiny bowl of porridge. "Oh, how lovely!" she exclaimed. "This is perfect – not too hot and not too cold." Goldilocks ladled the lovely porridge into her mouth, hardly pausing for breath. When she had licked the bowl clean, she placed the spoon back into the bowl.

Happy now that her tummy wasn't rumbling anymore, Goldilocks began to explore the rest of the cottage. It was very comfortable and reminded her of her own home. She began to wonder who lived in such a lovely house.

In the sitting room, on the mantelpiece above the little fire, there were photographs in beautifully carved wooden frames. "I wonder if they live here?" she muttered to herself. Peering up at the pictures, she noticed that they were of a family. A family of bears! A daddy bear, a mummy bear and a little tiny baby bear.

A little fearful now, she called out again, "Hello, is there anybody at home?" Again, nobody answered. Shrugging her shoulders, she sat down on the largest of the three chairs that were in the room. "My, this is far too big and hard for me," she said, as she tried to get comfortable. So, instead, she slipped off it and tried the medium-sized chair. "Oh dear, this one is far too soft," she grumbled.

Finally, she tried the smallest chair. It was perfect. Goldilocks sat back with a sigh. "How lovely," she said, smiling.

Suddenly, there was a loud cracking noise and the little chair collapsed beneath her. Picking herself up, she gathered the pieces of wood and tried to put it back together… but it was well and truly broken. She brushed the dust from her dress and hurriedly left the sitting room.

In the hallway, the front door was still open. The winding staircase, opposite the door, wound its way up into the darkness. Goldilocks didn't like the dark very much, but her curiosity got the better of her. She wondered who or what was upstairs.

Slowly she began to climb the stairs. They creaked and they groaned. It sounded very loud in the quiet cottage. At the top of the stairs, there were two doors. One door led into a huge bathroom. Inside there was a bath the size of a fish pond and a hand basin. She turned around and faced the other door.

Slowly she pushed it open. It creaked just like the stairs had done. Goldilocks stepped through the doorway. She found herself in a very big bedroom with three beds in it. They all had multicoloured patchwork quilts spread out on top of them.

Stretching and yawning, Goldilocks suddenly felt quite tired. She looked at her watch and saw that she'd been away from home for several hours. "I think I'll have a little sleep before I head back home," she sighed.

She climbed up onto the big bed and lay down. "Ouch, this bed is far too hard!" she cried. The mattress was as stiff as a plank. Jumping off the bed, Goldilocks clambered onto the medium-sized bed. "Oh dear, this bed is far too soft for me!" she squeaked, as she sank into the middle of the bed. The poor girl had to roll to the edge of the mattress to get off it.

Straightening her clothes and re-tying the ribbons in her hair, Goldilocks turned to the last bed in the far corner of the room. It was in front of a large window. It looked very small indeed. She sat down gently and tested the mattress. "Oh my, this is absolutely perfect," she sighed. Goldilocks rested her head back onto the lovely fluffy pillow and closed her eyes. "I'll just have a nap and then I'll go home," she mumbled. Within a matter of moments, she was fast asleep.

Daddy Bear, Mummy Bear and Baby Bear took off their Wellington boots, and left them outside the big, blue front door. They had just popped out to the local beehive to buy some honey. Daddy Bear was carrying a very large potful.

Earlier that morning, the family of bears had sat down for their breakfast of porridge when Mummy Bear realised that they had run out of honey.

"Not to worry," said Daddy Bear, cheerfully. "The porridge looks very hot. Why don't we all go and get some more honey?" Baby Bear clapped his hands together. He was pleased that they were going to get some more. He didn't like his porridge without a large swirl of the syrupy stuff on top of it.

Glad to be home again, Daddy Bear rubbed his tummy and ambled into the kitchen. He was very hungry now after the walk to the beehive and back.

He licked his lips and sat down at the large wooden table. "What's this?" he said frowning.

His spoon was already in his bowl of porridge and not lying on the table by the side of it, where it usually was. "Who's been eating my porridge?" he growled. He peered down into his large bowl, then up at Mummy Bear.

Mummy Bear looked at her bowl of porridge and gasped, "Who's been eating my porridge?" Her spoon was also in her bowl.

"Who's been eating my porridge?" howled Baby Bear. He picked up his bowl and held it out to his parents. "Look, they've eaten it all up. They've even licked the bowl clean!"

The poor bears wandered through into the sitting room. Mummy Bear stopped and gasped. Someone had been in there!

"Who's been sitting in my chair?" growled Daddy Bear. The cushion that he rested his back against was lying on the floor.

"Who's been sitting in my chair?" whispered Mummy Bear. There was a dip in the seat where someone had been sitting on it.

"Who's been sitting in my chair?" cried Baby Bear. "Look, they've smashed it to pieces."

Daddy Bear was not happy that someone had been into the cottage without being invited. "I'm going to check upstairs," he growled to Mummy Bear. He climbed the creaky staircase, two steps at a time. Mummy Bear and Baby Bear clambered up after him. At the top, Daddy Bear stepped into the bathroom. There was nobody there.

He turned to Mummy Bear and Baby Bear and put his finger to his lips, "Shhh!" They both nodded their heads. They all peeped around the corner of the bedroom door. Daddy Bear took a step inside.

"Who's been sleeping in my bed?" he demanded. The multicoloured patchwork quilt was all wrinkled where someone had been lying on it.

"Who's been sleeping in my bed?" gasped Mummy Bear. She dashed over to her bed and straightened her multicoloured patchwork quilt. Someone had been climbing on her bed too.

Baby Bear tugged on Mummy Bear's apron and pointed to his little bed beside the big window. "Look," he whispered, "that's who's been sleeping in your bed… and now they're sleeping in mine!"

The three bears crept up to Baby Bear's bed to get a closer look at their uninvited guest. Goldilocks was still fast asleep.

"It's only a little girl," said Mummy Bear, smiling. She looked at Daddy Bear who still looked very angry. "Stop frowning, Daddy Bear," she whispered, "You'll scare the poor child if she wakes." Mummy Bear reached out a paw and gently pushed a lock of hair out of Goldilocks' face.

Just then, Goldilocks woke up. She rubbed her eyes and then looked down at her wristwatch. "I should get home to Mummy now," she said to herself. "Oh my!" she shrieked when she saw the three bears peering down at her. Her scream made the bears jump and they all took a step away from Baby Bear's bed.

"Don't be frightened, little girl," said Mummy Bear kindly, but it was as if Goldilocks hadn't heard her. She was petrified! She hopped off the bed and ran out of the bedroom, down the creaky wooden stairs and out of the big, blue front door. She had to leap over the three pairs of Wellington boots in the doorway.

She ran as fast as her little legs would carry her, through the bushes and amongst the trees. She didn't stop until she got back home.

"Hello Goldilocks," said her mother. "Have you had a nice day, dear?" she called out from the kitchen.

Goldilocks rushed into the cosy kitchen and hugged her mother tightly. "Why, whatever is the matter, dear?" she asked. She picked up her daughter and carried her into the sitting room. She sat down on the large sofa, with Goldilocks on her lap. "Now, tell me what's the matter," she said softly.

Goldilocks told her mother what had happened in the woods, at the three bears' house.

"What have I told you about walking in the woods?" she said crossly.

"That I am not allowed to go too far into the woods, Mummy," mumbled Goldilocks.

She clung onto her mother and peeped towards the door, scared that at any moment a big grizzly bear would appear.

"What have I told you about going into a stranger's house?" asked her mother.

"That I am not allowed to go inside a stranger's house alone," mumbled Goldilocks again.

She looked up at her mother through tearful eyes. "I am ever so sorry. I promise I won't do it ever again, Mummy."

"There, there," said her mother. "Very well, let this be a lesson to you my child." She hugged the little girl tightly. She was sure that Goldilocks would never stray too far from home ever again.

THE END

Cinderella

Once upon a time the wife of a rich man fell very ill and died. His daughter went every day to her mother's grave and wept. In the winter, snow covered the grave under a thick blanket of white. When the snow melted and spring came, the girl's father married again. His new wife and her two daughters were jealous of the girl, who was much prettier than they were. "We'll put her to work in the kitchen to keep her out of sight," the stepmother decided. "In that case, she doesn't need these fine clothes," crowed the first sister. "Or these necklaces or ribbons in her hair," chanted the second gleefully. They took away all the girl's pretty things and dressed her in rags. Then the stepmother set her to work, tending the fire and cooking, washing and mending, and when all the work was done she found still more work for her to do.

The sisters took the girl's bedroom so the poor thing lay down exhausted in the cinders and the ashes to sleep, where she was always covered in dust. The sisters jeered at her, "Look, here comes Cinderella, princess of the cinders!" they shrieked. In her head, but not to their faces, Cinderella called them the 'ugly sisters' because they were so horrid.

One day, Cinderella's father had to go on a journey. "Oh, papa, bring us back some fine silk dresses," pleaded the first ugly sister. "Oh, papa, bring us back some jewels that flash like fire," pleaded the other one. "What shall I bring for you?" her father asked Cinderella. "Please bring me the first branch that touches your hat as you head for home," said Cinderella. The stepmother sneered and the ugly sisters screeched with laughter. "That's a stupid thing to wish for," they cried.

When the father returned he brought silk dresses and jewels that flashed like fire for the two ugly sisters. For Cinderella he brought a hazel branch which was the first branch that had touched his hat as he headed for home. Cinderella ran outside with her branch and planted it on her mother's grave. Then she wept so hard that she watered the branch with her tears. Soon the branch began to grow. Every day that Cinderella visited the grave she saw that something miraculous was happening. First, buds formed, then they opened and leaves unfurled. Soon the branch had turned into a little tree with branches of its own that waved in the wind. Birds came and perched in it; turtle doves, sparrows, and wrens. Cinderella talked to the tree and she talked to the birds, and the birds sang back to her.

One day a letter came that caused a great commotion in the household. "Mama, mama!" cried the first ugly sister, "we've been invited to a ball!" "It's an invitation from the prince," screamed the other one, snatching the letter for herself. "Calm down, my darlings, or you will faint!" commanded the stepmother. She took the letter from them and read it out. It was indeed an invitation to all the young ladies of the kingdom, to a ball the likes of which had never been seen before – a grand candlelit buffet and dance that would last three nights. After three nights the prince would choose his bride. "Just think, my dear," the stepmother simpered to her husband, "the prince is bound to choose one of my darling girls. Oh, what a triumph it will be!"

From that day on, the ball was in everyone's thoughts. The ugly sisters squabbled so much over what they would wear that Cinderella was ordered to sew new ball gowns for both of them, but nothing she did seemed right when they looked in the mirror.

The first night of the ball soon came round. "Now do our hair," demanded the ugly sisters, "make us beautiful for the prince." This was difficult indeed, but Cinderella did what she could. When the ugly sisters were putting the final touches to their make-up, Cinderella said to her stepmother, "What shall I wear to the ball?"

The three of them looked at her with wide-open eyes. "Why should you go to the ball?" asked the stepmother, aghast. "The invitation was to all the young ladies of the kingdom," said Cinderella, "please let me go." The stepmother frowned. Then she had an idea. She threw a bowl of rice in the ashes. "Pick up all the grains of rice and put them back in the bowl, then you can go to the ball." Cinderella would never be able to do it in time. Laughing, the three of them left the room. Cinderella knew exactly what to do. She ran straight outside to her hazel tree and called up to it, "Help me, help me, hazel tree."

Instantly the air was full of chirruping and cooing as sparrows and wrens and turtle doves followed Cinderella back to the kitchen and pecked among the ashes until they had picked up every grain of rice and put it back in the bowl.

Cinderella hurried with the bowl to her stepmother. "I have done what you asked," she said. "Now, please may I go to the ball?" The stepmother's face froze. "How can you go to the ball?" she said icily. "You have nothing to wear."

Cinderella begged and begged, but her stepmother had another idea. This time she threw two bowls of lentils into the ashes and said to Cinderella, "Pick up all the lentils and put them back in the bowls, then you can go to the ball." Cinderella would never do it in time.

Cinderella ran straight out to her hazel tree, calling, "Help me, help me, hazel tree." Again, sparrows and wrens and turtle doves flew down and followed her into the kitchen. They pecked up all the lentils in double quick time and Cinderella hurried to her stepmother. "I have done what you asked," she said, showing her the two full bowls. "Now, please may I go to the ball?" The stepmother's face darkened with fury. "Come, my darlings," she called to the ugly sisters, "we are leaving for the ball right now and this wretch will stay behind." With that, they got into the father's carriage, which was waiting at the door, and sped off, leaving Cinderella with only the birds to comfort her. The birds led Cinderella out into the garden and perched in the hazel tree. Cinderella knelt down and murmured sadly, "Help me, help me, hazel tree."

To Cinderella's surprise, the birds whirled up in a cloud of wing beats, and as they fluttered softly back down to earth she saw that, between them, they were carrying a beautiful gossamer-light dress embroidered with seed pearls, and a pair of satin slippers to match. Cinderella put them on and ran all the way to the ball.

The prince's palace was lit with a thousand candles. The dancing throng parted to let Cinderella through. No one recognised the humble serving girl, not even her family, and everyone agreed the stranger was the most beautiful young lady at the ball. The prince bowed and asked her to dance. He was so enchanted with her beauty that he refused to be parted from her all evening. When Cinderella saw her father leave, however, she slipped away.

Cinderella didn't want the prince to know she was just a kitchen maid, and when she saw his servant chasing after her, she hid in her father's barn. The prince's servant called at the house and begged permission to search the barn, but Cinderella had escaped through another door and run to her hazel tree. There she changed back into her rags. By the time her father came back indoors, she was lying in her place among the cinders.

The next night, after the ugly sisters, her father and stepmother had left for the ball, Cinderella ran out to the hazel tree and sang, "Help me, help me, hazel tree." There was a whirring of wings and the birds flew down, bringing an even more beautiful dress than the one before, embroidered with sapphires and silver thread, with sapphire slippers to match. Cinderella put them on and hurried to the ball.

The prince was waiting for her and again they danced together all night. When her father left, Cinderella slipped away. With the prince's servant following her, she scrambled up the big old pear tree in her father's garden. While the servant was pounding at the door to call her father, Cinderella jumped out of the tree. She ran to her hazel tree, put on her rags and went to lie in her place by the fire. Her father chopped down the pear tree at the servant's request. Of course, no one was found in its branches. He wondered why the beautiful princess would want to hide twice in his garden.

On the third night Cinderella was left alone, as usual. She ran out to her tree and sang joyfully, "Help me, help me, hazel tree." Again the sky was filled with birds, this time bringing her the most beautiful dress of all. It was spun in threads of the purest gold, with golden slippers to match. Cinderella put on the dress and slippers and she looked so beautiful that all the birds broke out in song. She ran to the ball, where the prince was waiting.

When her father left, Cinderella fled, but in her haste she lost one of her slippers. The prince's servant brought it to him and the prince kissed it, declaring, "This delicate golden slipper belongs to the princess who has won my heart. I will search all the land until I find her, for she is the one I will marry."

The next day the prince's royal coach set out, with the golden slipper placed on a velvet cushion on the seat. The prince's servant knocked at the door of every household in the land and offered the slipper to any young lady living there, in the hope of finding the mystery princess. But the slipper didn't fit anyone. Finally, the royal coach arrived at Cinderella's house. The ugly sisters were quarrelling over who should try the slipper first. "Don't argue, my beauties," hushed the stepmother. "You both have such exquisite feet, the slipper is bound to fit one of you." She winked and pushed her first daughter forward. The ugly sister squeezed and she squirmed and she pushed, until she had crammed her foot into the slipper.

Her mother was jubilant. "We have found your royal bride," she called to the servant, who set off for the palace at once with the ugly sister inside the coach. As they passed the hazel tree, a strange thing happened. All the birds – sparrows, wrens and turtle doves – rose from the tree in a great cloud and sang:

"This is not the real princess!
Look at the slipper – what a mess!"

The servant stopped and looked at the slipper, and sure enough he found that the ugly sister's foot had swollen so much that the slipper had flown off. So he took the girl back home and asked to see her sister.

The second ugly sister took the slipper and tried to make it fit. She spread her toes and pushed in her foot as far as it would go, but her foot just would not fill the slipper.

"Your heel is too small," spat the stepmother crossly. "Wrap some bandages around your foot when the servant isn't looking." So, while the servant was talking, the ugly sister had bandages wrapped around her foot. She put on the shoe and it fitted perfectly. Her mother was relieved. "Here is your royal bride," she called to the servant, who set off for the palace at once with the ugly sister inside the coach. As they passed the hazel tree, the same thing happened as before. The sparrows, the wrens and the turtle doves flew up from the tree in a cloud and sang:

"This isn't the princess – she's a fake!
Look in the slipper before it's too late!"

Again, the servant stopped and looked in the slipper, and he found it was full of bandages. So he took the girl back home. "Do you have any other daughters?" he asked Cinderella's father.

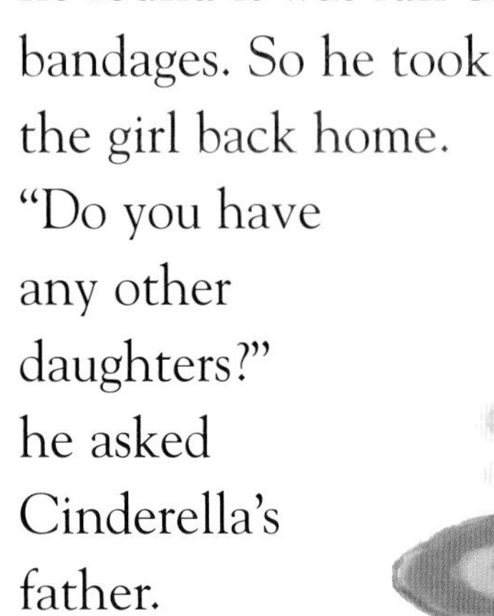

"Well, no," said the father nervously, but Cinderella had stood up from her place in the ashes and was walking towards them. "Except, that is, for Cinderella."

The servant looked at Cinderella and felt sure that he had seen her somewhere before. She sat down on a stool and he held out the golden slipper. Her foot slid inside it without any effort at all. So the servant took Cinderella back to the palace and, even though her hair was matted, her face and hands dirty, and her dress old and ragged, the prince recognised her at once as the beautiful girl he had danced with each night at the ball. He went down on bended knee before her and asked for her hand in marriage.

As you may guess, Cinderella accepted him.

There was a wonderful wedding in the land and, as the happy couple processed to the palace, the train of Cinderella's wedding dress was carried by the birds from the hazel tree, who accompanied the prince and princess all their lives with their glorious singing.

As for the stepmother and the ugly sisters, they stayed at home, crying their eyes out and rubbing their feet, and vowing never to be horrible to anyone ever again.

THE END

Snow White

Once upon a time, on a freezing winter's day, a beautiful queen sat at her window working on her embroidery. As she sewed she fell into a daydream. Outside the castle, snow was falling, making a soft, white carpet on the ground. A raven landed on the branch of a tree.

"How I would love to have a daughter," thought the queen. Just at that moment she pricked her finger and three drops of ruby red blood welled up and spilled like tears. Looking down at her finger, she thought, "If I were to have a daughter, she would have skin as white and soft as the driven snow, hair as black and shiny as the raven's wings and lips as ruby red as blood." Then the queen said aloud, "I would call her Snow White."

In time, the queen's wish was granted and she gave birth to a beautiful baby girl.

When Snow White was born, however, the queen fell terribly ill and died. It wasn't long before the king married again, but the new queen was not a good mother to Snow White. She left her to be brought up by the servants.

The new queen was a woman of striking looks and considerable vanity. Every day, she looked into her magic mirror and asked:

"Mirror, mirror, on the wall,
who is the fairest of us all?"

The mirror replied:

"Oh queen, you are the
fairest in all the land."

Satisfied with the mirror's answer, the queen would go happily about her business.

When Snow White was seven years old, however, the queen gazed admiringly into her mirror and, once more, asked it who was fairest. To her horror, the mirror replied:

"Oh queen, you are a beauty,
it's true, but Snow White has
grown much fairer than you."

"Yaaargh!" screamed the queen, flinging her hairbrush at the mirror.

The queen stormed off to find Snow White who was playing in the garden. Watching her through the window, the queen knew that the mirror spoke the truth. The child was truly beautiful. She had skin as white and soft as the driven snow, her hair was as black and shiny as a raven's wings and her lips were as ruby red as blood. "This is quite insupportable!" spat the queen, twisting her handkerchief in her fingers. "I must have the girl killed forthwith."

Striding through the castle, the queen went straight to the huntsman. "Take Snow White away this minute," she ordered. "Take her into the forest and kill her. Bring me her heart so I can be sure she's dead."

The huntsman took Snow White by the hand and led her into the forest, but he knew he couldn't do what the queen had asked.

Instead, the huntsman left Snow White alone in the forest and, on his way back to the castle, killed a wild boar with his bow and arrow and cut out its heart.

When the huntsman gave the heart to the queen, her cheeks turned pink with pleasure and she felt sure that she would be the fairest in the land once more.

Back in the forest, Snow White was lost and afraid. She wandered further and further from the path. She tripped over tree roots and brambles scratched her and caught in her hair. Suddenly, she came to a clearing, and in the clearing stood a cottage. Snow White knocked at the door, but no one answered. She cautiously lifted the latch and went inside.

Show White saw a fire ready to be lit, a table with seven places laid for supper and seven chairs waiting to be sat on. She tried each of the chairs in turn. One was too high and one was too low. One was too hard and one was too soft. One was too big and one was too small. But one was just right. For every chair she sat on, there was a plate of supper on the table waiting to be eaten. Snow White tried a forkful from each and felt much better.

Snow White went upstairs where, in the bedroom, she found seven beds waiting to be slept in with their covers turned back invitingly. She lay down on each of the beds in turn. One was too high and one was too low. One was too hard and one was too soft. One was too big and one was too small. But one was just right. She lay down and fell soundly asleep.

Later on, when it grew dark, the owners of the cottage came home for their supper. They had been working down a mine all day, cutting precious stones from the rock with their pickaxes, and they were tired and hungry. When they entered their cottage, they immediately felt that things were not quite as they should be.

"Well, singe my whiskers!" said one of them. "Someone has taken a bite of my supper!"

"Mine too!" gasped a second. "Mine too! Mine too!" chorused the others.

They were too tired from their hard day's work to mind too much, so they sat down and ate, then went up to bed.

"Well, singe my whiskers!" exclaimed the first one. "Someone's been sleeping in my bed!"

"And mine!" yelped a second. "Hush!" whispered a third, "Someone is asleep in my bed!"

They all gathered around to look and saw that the intruder was a beautiful little girl. They didn't want to disturb her so they left her where she was, sleeping peacefully.

The following morning, Snow White woke to find the seven miners eating breakfast. They were dwarfs, no bigger than she was.

"Well, singe my whiskers!" said the first dwarf. "Look who's awake!"

They all put their spoons down with a clatter and stared at Snow White.

"No need to be afraid of us," said the second dwarf, "but tell us who you are and what brings you here."

The dwarfs made a place for Snow White at the table and gave her a bowl of porridge. She told them the story of how her stepmother, the wicked queen, had made the huntsman take her into the forest and how he had spared her life rather than take her heart back to the castle.

The dwarfs muttered to each other and tugged at their beards, then one of them said, "You must never go back to the castle. Stay here and make your home with us. In return, you can keep the cottage neat and clean and cook our meals."

Delighted, Snow White agreed.

Snow White was very happy in her new home because the seven dwarfs were very kind to her. Although she had never done any cooking and cleaning before (she was a princess after all), she learned quickly and enjoyed her work.

Back at the castle, the queen was happy too, with no one to challenge her beauty. One day, she confidently consulted her mirror:

"Mirror, mirror, on the wall,
who is the fairest of us all?"

To her horror, the mirror replied:

"Oh queen, you are a beauty, it's true,
but Snow White is far, far fairer than you."

The queen flew into a rage. "Impossible!" she shrieked, "I had the wretch killed!"

The next morning the queen wrapped a big shawl around her and disguised herself as a pedlar. Carrying a basket of trinkets, she set off to the forest to find Snow White. Soon, the queen came to a clearing where she saw a neat little cottage. She knocked at the door. Now, Snow White had promised the seven dwarfs that she would never open the door to a stranger, but as she peeked through the window and saw the old pedlar woman, she decided to let her in.

"Look at these pretty trinkets, my dear," said the queen in a cracked voice, as she spread the baubles and beads on the table. Snow White picked out a necklace and held it up. "See how it sparkles, my dear," croaked the queen in her disguise. "Let me fasten it around your neck." The queen took the necklace and pulled it so tightly around Snow White's neck that the poor girl fell down in a faint. The queen gave a triumphant shriek. "Dead! Dead at last!" she cried. She hurried back to the palace, very pleased with the way her day had turned out.

When darkness fell, the seven dwarfs arrived home from the mine. "Singe my whiskers!" said the first one. "Why is Snow White lying on the floor?" Quickly, the dwarfs released the necklace from around her neck, stroked her hair and gave her a hot drink.

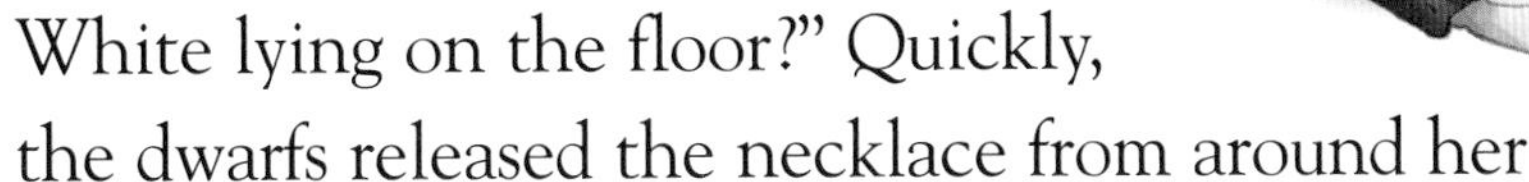

"It was no pedlar woman who did this," muttered the dwarfs to one another, "it was the wicked queen." They made Snow White promise again that she would never, ever open the door to let anyone in.

The next day, the queen dressed in her finest gown and put on her most precious jewels. Smelling of sweet perfume, she went to consult her mirror:

"Mirror, mirror, on the wall,
who is the fairest of us all?"

To her horror, the mirror replied:

"Oh queen, you are a beauty, it's true,
but Snow White is far, far fairer than you."

The queen was incredulous, indignant and infuriated. "What! Still not dead?" she spat. The queen spent the rest of the day making plans.

The following morning, the queen left the castle dressed as a countrywoman, her face hidden under the wide brim of her hat. She went straight to the cottage in the clearing and rapped at the door.

Snow White remembered her promise to the dwarfs and refused to open the door, but she thought it would be safe to open the window.

"I'm on my way to market, my dear," said the queen, brightly, "and it's such a hot day. Could I trouble you for a drink of water?" Snow White fetched a glass of water and handed it through the window. The queen drank it down in one gulp. "Now, let me give you a little present to thank you, my dear," she said. She reached in her basket and took out a glistening comb that she'd laced with poison. "Let me run it through your lovely raven hair," said the queen. Just as the comb touched Snow White's hair, the poor girl fell down in a faint.

Now, when the seven dwarfs came home that night, they were most distressed to find Snow White on the floor again.

"Singe my whiskers!" said the first one as he gently took the comb from her hair.

The dwarfs clustered around Snow White and sighed with relief as she opened her eyes. When Snow White told them her story, the dwarfs muttered amongst themselves. "It wasn't a countrywoman who did this, it was the wicked queen," they said. "Never, ever open the door or the window to anyone," they told her, and Snow White promised that she would be careful.

Back in the castle, the queen was jubilant. She rushed to the mirror and asked:

"Mirror, mirror, on the wall,
who is the fairest of us all?"

To her absolute amazement the mirror replied:

"Oh queen, you are a beauty, it's true, but Snow White is far, far fairer than you."

This time there was no limit to the queen's fury. "I must stop this torture," she cried. "I must get rid of that wretched girl once and for all."

The next day, the queen took a beautiful big apple, green one side and red the other. She put some poison in the red side, then she disguised herself as an old man, with a hat pulled well down over her eyes. She hobbled off to the cottage in the clearing and rapped at the window.

"Open up, my dear," said the queen in a gruff voice. "I want to give you this apple."

"I don't accept gifts from strangers," replied Snow White.

"Never mind," said the queen, as she took a big bite from the green side of the apple. "I'll leave the best part for you to eat," she said, putting it on the windowsill. With that, she shuffled off into the forest.

As soon as Snow White was alone, she opened the window and picked up the apple. She took a big bite from the red side and immediately fell to the ground.

When the seven dwarfs came home that night and found Snow White lying stone cold on the floor, they were inconsolable. "She really is dead this time! Our beautiful Snow White is dead!" they wept.

The dwarfs built a beautiful glass coffin for Snow White, who didn't look dead at all – her skin was still as white as snow, her hair as black as a raven's wings and her lips as ruby red as blood. They gently laid her body inside the coffin and filled it with flowers, then they carried it to the top of the hill where they could visit every day.

Seven years later, as the dwarfs climbed the hill, they saw a handsome prince sitting beside the coffin. He was gazing in rapture at Snow White's beautiful face. The prince asked the dwarfs' permission to lift the lid of the coffin so he could kiss Snow White. The dwarfs took pity on the love-struck prince, so they agreed. As the prince lifted the lid, the coffin slipped and everyone gasped as the jolt sent the piece of poisoned apple shooting from Snow White's throat!

Snow White coughed and sat up. The dwarfs cheered and hugged one another and, as Snow White gazed at the prince, he asked her to marry him. Snow White agreed.

A grand wedding was arranged to which everyone was invited, including Snow White's stepmother, the wicked queen. On the day of the wedding the queen went to her mirror and asked:

"Mirror, mirror, on the wall,
who is the fairest of us all?"

To her astonishment the mirror replied:

"Oh queen, you are a beauty, it's true,
but the prince's bride is fairer than you."

The queen turned pale and flung the mirror to the floor, smashing it into a million pieces. She hurried to the palace to get a glimpse of the bride. When she saw it was Snow White, looking lovelier than ever, she ran screaming into the forest and was never seen again.

As for Snow White and her handsome prince – they lived happily ever after.

THE END

Rumpelstiltskin

Once upon a time

there was a miller whose job was to grind wheat into flour. He sent this flour to the king whose bakers turned it into the finest bread in all the land.

The miller was very proud that he worked for the king, but this honour had made him rather boastful. One day, the miller found himself in the king's company. Not wanting to miss an opportunity to impress the king, he urgently tried to think of something to say.

"Did you know, Your Majesty," he began, "that I have a beautiful grown-up daughter at home?"

"Hmm," replied the king, not really listening.

"She has the most amazing gift," continued the miller, desperate for the king's attention. "She can turn straw into gold!"

"Really?" said the king, suddenly very interested indeed.

Now that the miller had the king's full attention, he had to think quickly. Every house had a spinning wheel, that was used to make thread to weave into cloth, and the image of someone spinning was the first thing that popped into the miller's head.

"Sire," said the miller, "my daughter uses a spinning wheel to turn ordinary strands of straw into glittering threads of gold!"

Of course, it was quite untrue. Such a thing is just not possible, but the miller didn't care. All he wanted was to impress the king.

"Your daughter's gift is truly amazing!" exclaimed the king. "Bring her to the palace so I can watch her at work."

The miller wished more than anything that he hadn't lied, but he had no choice... he had to obey the king. Later that day, the miller took his daughter to the palace.

The king watched as the miller and his daughter approached.

"You may return tomorrow morning to collect your daughter," he told the miller as he led the nervous-looking girl inside. The king took her through a labyrinth of twisting corridors until they came to a set of enormous doors. Opening the doors, the miller's daughter gasped as she saw a room full of straw and a spinning wheel in the centre.

"There you are, dear," said the king, smiling at the frightened young girl. "I'd like you to turn all this straw into gold by tomorrow morning… or you will go to prison for the rest of your life!"

CLUNK! The door was shut and bolted and the miller's daughter found herself alone in the room.

"What am I going to do?" she wailed, bursting into tears and sobbing into her handkerchief.

Suddenly, a little man popped out from behind the door.

"Why are you crying, young lady?" asked the tiny stranger.

"The king has commanded me to spin all this straw into gold by tomorrow morning," wailed the girl, "and I have no idea how to do it. The king will be furious when he finds out my father lied and I'll be sent to prison for the rest of my life."

"We can't have that now, can we?" cried the little man. "I will spin all this straw into gold in return for the pretty necklace you are wearing."

Even though the necklace had been given to her by her mother for her sixteenth birthday, the startled girl tore it off and handed it to the little man. Then she lay down on a bale of straw where the gentle hum of the spinning wheel soon sent her to sleep. She didn't even stir when the little man gently moved her to spin the straw on which she lay into gold as well.

Next morning, when the miller's daughter awoke, a dazzling light made her cover her eyes. Instead of bales of straw, the room was stacked to the ceiling with giant reels of sparkling gold thread. The miller's daughter looked around, but there was no sign of her mysterious helper. Before she had time to take in the scene, the door was thrown open and in marched the king.

"So it is true!" he cried, looking at the glittering reels of thread in delight.

The miller scratched his head in amazement and blew out his cheeks with relief – thank goodness his pretty daughter would not be thrown into prison.

Just as the miller and his daughter turned to go, the king put an arm around each of them.

"Come back this evening, my friends," he said. "I'd like to see you perform this miracle again!"

That night, the poor young girl found herself locked in a much bigger room with another spinning wheel and even more bales of straw piled from floor to ceiling.

"I pray that little man appears again," she murmured. "Your prayers are answered!" he cried, popping out from behind the spinning wheel as if by magic.

Once again, the little man wanted payment for his work, so the girl gave him the ring from her finger.

Although it was a present from her father on her eighteenth birthday, it seemed much more important to keep the little man happy.

The miller's daughter slept through the night on a bale of straw once more, while the strange little figure sat bent over the spinning wheel, focussed on his work.

When the girl awoke the next morning, the little man had gone and every single piece of straw had been turned into precious gold. By now, the king had plenty of gold, but he was greedy and wanted more.

He called the miller's daughter back for a third time and led her to an enormous barn that was almost bursting with bales of straw. There was only just room for a spinning wheel tucked behind the gigantic doors.

"This is the last time I'm going to ask you to do this," said the king, "but this time, the rules are slightly different. As before, if you fail to turn all this straw into gold, I will send you to prison forever, but if you succeed, I should like to marry you and make you my queen! You will never have to spin straw into gold again!"

That night, the little man appeared before her for the third time, but when the worried girl saw him she burst into floods of tears.

"I have nothing to give you for tonight's work!" she sobbed.

"Nothing?" he queried, frowning up at her.

"No, nothing at all!" she replied.

"In that case," said the little man, "you must make me a promise. If I do as you want and the king marries you, you must give me your first baby as soon as it is born!"

"Agreed!" cried the girl. She knew it was silly to make such a promise, but what else could she do?

Filled with relief, the miller's daughter drifted to sleep on one of the many bales, while the little man sat at the spinning wheel, working harder than ever to turn the straw into reels of shimmering gold.

The following morning, the king unlocked the barn doors to reveal reels and reels of shining gold. He stepped forward, clasped the girl in his arms and asked her to marry him. The miller's daughter agreed, much to the delight of her father, whose lie to the king could have lost him his daughter for ever!

The day the miller's daughter married the king was the happiest of her life! Everyone in the kingdom came to watch and cheer the happy couple as they started their life together as man and wife. As the weeks passed, the new queen forgot about her promise to the funny little man.

Exactly one year after her marriage, the queen gave birth to a baby boy.

The following day, as she rocked the sleeping infant in her arms, the little man appeared in her bedroom.

"Give the baby to me," he snarled. "You made a promise, remember!"

The queen looked horrified. "You cannot mean this!" she cried. "Let me give you something else instead."

The queen offered money, jewels, fine horses, houses, land – all the best things she could think of in her husband's kingdom.

Each time, however, the little man shook his head.

"Why offer me riches when I can spin straw into gold?" he argued. "I want more than money. I want your baby!"

The queen sobbed and sobbed, holding her baby tightly in her arms, but the little man just stared at her, saying nothing. Eventually, the visitor decided to give the queen one more chance.

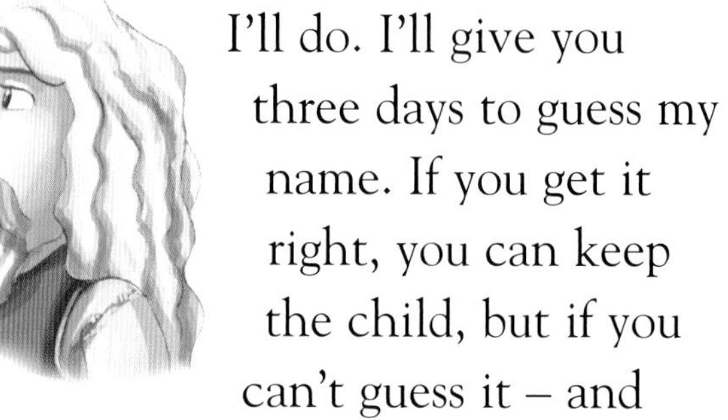

"Listen," he whispered, moving so close to her she could smell his musty breath. "I'll tell you what I'll do. I'll give you three days to guess my name. If you get it right, you can keep the child, but if you can't guess it – and I'm sure you won't – then the baby's mine forever." With a cackle, the little man disappeared into thin air.

The queen had a book containing hundreds of first names, so she felt confident she would be able to guess the name of the little man.

When he arrived the next day, she began to read names from the book.

"Is your name Arthur, Albert or Andrew?" she asked.

"Nope!" replied the visitor.

"Bert, Barry or Brian, then?" continued the queen.

"Wrong again!" sang the little man.

The queen read out every name in the book until, finally, she cried, "I know! Your name's Zak!"

"No it isn't," laughed the tiny figure. "You've used up your first day. I'll be back tomorrow."

Sure enough, at exactly the same time the next day, the little man appeared in the queen's bedroom again.

"Well?" he inquired, "What's my name?"

The queen had spent all day in the castle library, copying down unusual names and even inventing some in the hope of guessing the right one. She went through the new list, saying, "You're called Nimrod, Littlefoot, Fairyfeet, Hairyfeet, Baggypants, Wobblebottom..." and so the list went on.

Every time the queen said a new name, the little man shook his head, skipping from one foot to the other.

"All wrong, queenie," he cackled. "I'll be back tomorrow – be ready to hand over your baby!"

That night, the queen did not go to bed. She walked up and down the castle corridors, hugging her precious baby to her chest. As she passed the kitchens, she heard two servants talking.

One of them said to the other, "A strange thing happened to me today. I was out in the forest, collecting mushrooms for the king's breakfast, when I saw a tiny hut with a big fire burning outside it. Dancing around the fire was a funny little man with a bushy white beard."

"He was singing a song that went like this:

'I shall bake bread and fine wine brew,
then, little prince, I'm coming for you!
There's no way the queen shall claim
that RUMPELSTILTSKIN is my name!'"

Smiling to herself, the queen hurried away. She tucked her son beneath the covers of his cot and went to bed herself, sleeping soundly throughout the night.

The next day, the little man arrived exactly on time. "This is your last chance, Ma'am!" he said, giving a low bow. "Guess my name, or your baby is mine!"

"Is your name Damien?" asked the queen.

"No," replied the visitor, starting to get excited.

"So, is it Wilfred?" the queen asked.

"No, no," chuckled the little man, getting even more excited.

"I can think of only one more name," continued the queen, "and that's Rumpelstiltskin!"

"ARRGH! Who told you?" screamed the little man, stamping his foot so hard with rage that it went right through the floorboards! Shaking his fists and shouting angrily, Rumpelstiltskin disappeared in a puff of smoke… and he was never seen again!

THE END

The Princess and the Pea

There was once a kingdom, in a country a long way from here, where a king and queen lived with their only son. The royal couple were getting on in years and realised it was time their son took on the responsibility of running the palace instead of lazing about or entertaining his friends. They really wanted him to find himself a wife and start acting as a future king should. The king and queen held lots of parties in the hope that the prince would choose a suitable bride, but no-one met with the prince's high expectations.

"I'm determined to marry only a real princess!" the prince announced firmly, "and, so far, I haven't met one."

"Then why don't you go out to explore the world?" asked the king, wearily. "A real princess is hardly likely to come knocking on the door." (Privately, the king thought his son was being just a bit too fussy. After all, his own wife had grown up in the kingdom next door and they had been happy for many years.) The prince eventually agreed with his father – he was rather bored with his life at home, anyway.

The next morning, the prince set off on a grand tour of the world. In every country he visited, he was invited to lunch parties, tea parties, dinner parties, grand balls and cocktail evenings, but nowhere did he find what he was looking for. Real princesses seemed to be in very short supply!

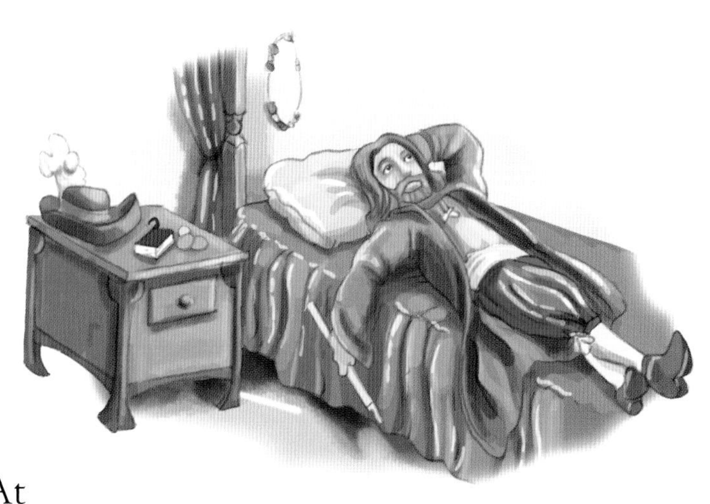

After several months, the prince returned from his tour fed up and worn out. He shut himself in his room, picked up his flute and played his favourite music very loudly. At this rate, he was going to remain a bachelor for the rest of his life and the kingdom would pass to his frightful cousin. The prince couldn't bear to think about it and wished he had started to look for a bride a bit sooner.

The king and queen were fed up, too. The prince's tour had cost the treasury an absolute fortune and there was nothing to show for it.

The weather didn't help, either. The wind howled around the palace eaves, rain lashed against the windows, hail rattled on the roof, whilst lightning flashed and thunder crashed.

The king and queen sat huddled close to the fire in their private parlour. They were wrapped in their warmest nightwear and wore cosy slippers on their feet.

Up in his room, the prince played his music louder still in order to drown out the sound of the storm. He didn't hear the knocking on the palace door. It was the old king himself who got up to answer it.

As soon as the door was opened, the force of the wind pushed it back into the king's face and almost flattened him against the wall! Outside, it was pitch black – the wind howled and whistled and the rain poured down in torrents.

The king peered into the darkness. "Hello? Is anyone there?" he shouted against the roar and crash of the storm. As he held up the candle he carried, he saw something wet and soggy on the doorstep. It moved...

"May I come in?" said the shape in the dark. "I just need to dry out a bit until the storm passes."

The king peered into the gloom. He could just make out the figure of a girl. Her hair was wet, rain ran from her skin, her clothes hung on her like wet dishcloths and her shoes squelched. She couldn't have been wetter.

"Come in, come in," said the shocked king. "This is not the weather to be outside. Come and dry yourself beside the fire, but tread carefully – this old palace is in need of some urgent repair."

The girl stepped carefully over the threshold and stood dripping on the cracked marbled tiles of the entrance hall. She took off her wet cloak and let it fall to the floor.

Looking around at the crumbling masonry, the girl said, "You must get in touch with my father's workmen. They've just repaired the roof above the throne room."

"Throne room?" repeated the king. "So you live in a palace, too?"

"Yes," replied the girl. "Bigger than this, actually. My father has taken over quite a few neighbouring counties and now rules over quite a large kingdom." The king rubbed his chin thoughtfully. Hope was rising in his heart and he quite forgot that the girl was still dripping wet.

"Your dad – um, father – is he, um, a king, then?" asked the king. "Yes," replied the girl. "Just like me, then!" chuckled the king. The girl glanced at the blanket wrapped around his shoulders and the fluffy slippers on his feet. "Well, sort of," she replied.

The king didn't notice the doubt in her voice. "So that makes you a princess, then?" he said, rubbing his hands together, gleefully. The princess nodded slowly and wondered just what kind of kingdom this was. This king certainly didn't act or dress like her father.

"So, um, what are you doing out on your own on such a terrible night?" asked the king.

"I'm on a quest to find a husband," the girl replied. "Not just any husband, you understand. Being a real princess myself, I'm not going to marry just anyone. No, he's got to be a prince, as well as someone I can admire and respect."

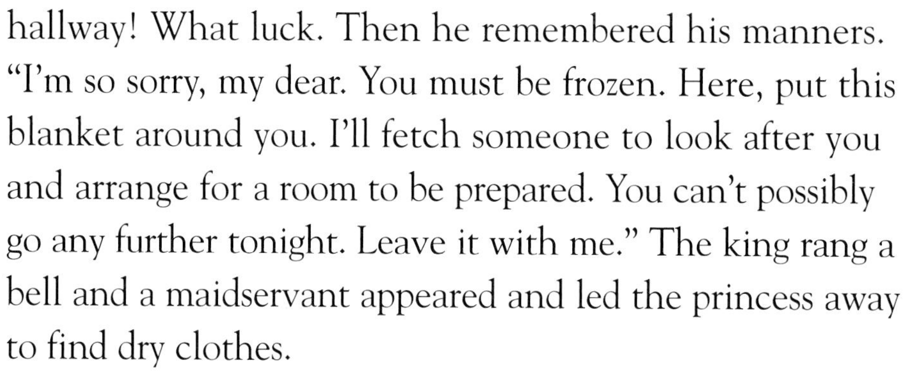

"Quite," said the king. He was feeling very excited now. A real princess! Here, in his hallway! What luck. Then he remembered his manners. "I'm so sorry, my dear. You must be frozen. Here, put this blanket around you. I'll fetch someone to look after you and arrange for a room to be prepared. You can't possibly go any further tonight. Leave it with me." The king rang a bell and a maidservant appeared and led the princess away to find dry clothes.

Hurrying briskly to the parlour, the king couldn't wait to tell his wife the good news. The queen, however, wasn't quite so ready to believe the girl's story.

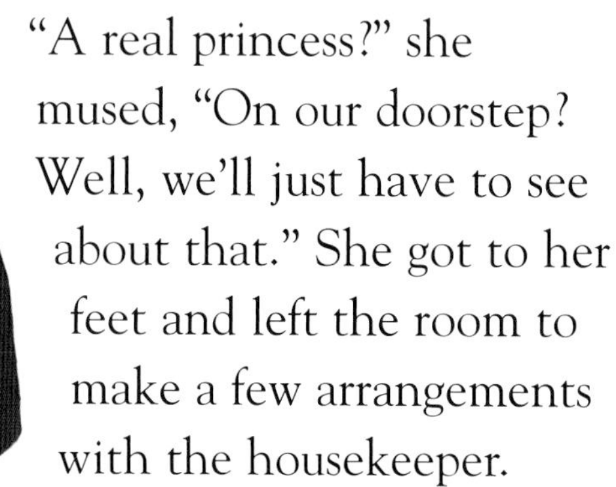

"A real princess?" she mused, "On our doorstep? Well, we'll just have to see about that." She got to her feet and left the room to make a few arrangements with the housekeeper.

Meanwhile, the prince had grown tired of playing his flute and was starting to feel less sorry for himself. He decided to join his parents for dinner. As he made his way along the corridor, he turned a corner and came face to face with a girl. Although her hair was damp and she was wearing a bathrobe, she was the most beautiful girl he'd ever seen. He'd certainly never seen her before – maybe she was a new maidservant.

Hearing him approach, the girl turned and said, "Excuse me, but I'm trying to find a bathroom. There are so many doors to choose from and I'm afraid I'm lost."

"Here," said the prince, "let me show you." He led the girl a little further along the corridor and opened a door.

"Thank you," she said, smiling. The prince smiled back. His stomach was turning somersaults and he felt strangely excited. He stood for a moment, staring at the closed bathroom door, having completely forgotten what it was he was on his way to do. Ah, yes. He was off to dinner with his parents. Maybe they would know who the new maidservant was.

As he entered the parlour, the prince found his father grinning from ear to ear.

"Why, there you are!" said the king. "We've got a surprise for you!"

The prince was instantly suspicious. "A surprise?" he asked.

"Yes!" replied his father, drawing him over to the fire. "We have a real princess here in the palace!"

"Oh, yes?" said the prince. His nice, fluttery feeling was suddenly replaced by heavy dread. "How do you know?"

"How do I know what?" asked the king, confused.

"How do you know she's a real princess? I suppose she told you."

"Well, yes, as a matter of fact…" said the king, but he saw the scorn in the prince's eyes so added, "anyway, your mother is… er… checking it out."

"Oh," said the prince. He was not comfortable with the idea of his parents interfering in his search for a suitable bride. No doubt they would try to foist anyone onto him, just to see him married. Besides, his need for a real princess suddenly didn't seem so important now that he had met the new maid.

"Is this real princess going to have dinner with us tonight?" asked the prince.

"Of course!" replied the king, brightening. "It will be an excellent chance for you to meet her."

The prince wasn't sure he wanted to meet anyone, princess or otherwise. He decided to go back upstairs to try to find the pretty maid instead.

"If you don't mind," he said, "I think I'll wait until the morning. I'm... ah..." he yawned, "very tired all of a sudden. Besides, I'm not really dressed suitably to have dinner with a visiting princess. Don't worry. I'll ask the kitchen staff to send up a tray."

"Oh, all right. Suit yourself," said the king. He was disappointed, but knew it was no good trying to force his son to do anything once he'd made up his mind. Besides, in the morning the princess might look a little less, well, wet.

Upstairs, meanwhile, the queen and the housekeeper had been very busy. They had been preparing a special bed for their guest. First, the queen ordered that the bed be stripped of all the bedclothes, then she placed a small, dried pea on the wooden base. The queen and the housekeeper then put twenty mattresses on top of the pea, followed by twenty feather beds on top of the mattresses.

"That should do it!" said the queen, standing back to admire her handiwork.

"Ahem, excuse me, Ma'am…" the housekeeper ventured.

"Yes?" replied the queen.

"How will the princess er…"

They both stared up at the swaying pile, which was towering above their heads.

"We'll have to give her a stepladder," said the queen.

"Very well, Ma'am," replied the housekeeper.

Satisfied, the queen went back downstairs to rejoin her husband in the parlour.

When the prince returned to his room, he noticed that the bathroom was empty and the girl had gone. He strolled up and down the corridor, hoping she might appear again, but he was to be disappointed. He wandered back to his room, deciding to make a point of visiting the servants' hall in the morning.

Meanwhile, the princess joined the king and queen for dinner, wearing a dress that the maidservant had found her.

After dinner, the queen took the princess to the bedroom that had been prepared earlier. When the princess saw the bed, with the stepladder alongside, she politely hid her surprise. Privately, she thought that the sooner she could leave this weird place, the better.

The following morning, the princess dressed and went downstairs to join the king and queen for breakfast.

"Good morning, my dear," said the queen. "Did you sleep well?" The princess pulled a face. "Well, no actually. I couldn't get comfortable. I'm afraid my bed had something extremely hard and knobbly in it. I'm black and blue with bruises."

The queen could hardly conceal her delight, but gave the king a long, meaningful glance and a nod. Only a real princess could have felt a small, dried pea under all those featherbeds and mattresses.

At that moment, the prince walked in, scowling. He had been down to the servants' hall very early, and although there were plenty of maids – under maids, kitchen maids, scullery maids, upstairs maids and downstairs maids – he had seen no sign of the new girl. In fact, when he pressed for information, the housekeeper told him that she had not taken on anyone new in the last two years.

"Mother," he began, "what's happened to that new maid?" Then he stopped, as he saw the princess seated at the table. "Oh, hello. It's you!" he exclaimed. He couldn't believe what he saw. Her hair was fine and golden. The prince thought it looked like rays of sunshine. Her eyes were as blue as spring forget-me-nots and her lips were the colour of ruby red roses.

The prince sighed. It was then he realised his mistake – a maid would never eat breakfast with his parents.

"Hello, again," said the princess, smiling radiantly.

A rather attractive blush came to her cheeks. As the prince gazed in rapture at the beautiful girl, he felt his own face grow hot.

"My dear," said the queen to her son, "this is the princess we told you about. You can be sure that she is very real indeed."

The prince took the girl by the hand and realised that he would love her for the rest of his life – princess or not.

THE END

Little Red Riding Hood

Once upon a time there was a little girl who lived with her mother and father in a beautiful cottage at the edge of a big, dark forest. Her father was a woodcutter and her friends were the forest creatures, for the little girl knew how to talk to the squirrels, the deer and the birds.

Every day, she rode her pony deep into the forest to visit her grandmother, who was very old and lived all alone. For the little girl's birthday, her grandmother had given her a beautiful red velvet cloak with a hood, which the little girl wore every time she was out riding her pony. In fact, the little girl wore her cloak so often that no-one could ever remember her name – they simply called her Little Red Riding Hood.

One day, just as Little Red Riding Hood was about to set off to visit her grandmother with a basket of good things to eat, she discovered that her pony was lame.

"You will have to walk to your grandmother's house today," said her mother, "so remember what I told you and don't speak to any strangers on the way."

Little Red Riding Hood nodded and looked inside the basket. Her mother had baked a fruitcake and wrapped it in a clean white cloth, there were six brown speckled eggs nestling in some hay and a fresh pat of butter in a dish. As she headed off with the basket towards her grandmother's house, Little Red Riding Hood heard her mother call out, "Remember to keep to the path!"

It wasn't long before Little Red Riding Hood was deep within the dark, green forest. Everything looked different now that she wasn't sitting high up on her pony. She saw a family of rabbits playing amongst the tall grass beneath the trees, so she crouched down to speak to them. Then a party of ants came marching past, so Little Red Riding Hood helped them carry a leaf to their home. Some time later, she found a baby bird that had fallen from its nest, so she lifted it up gently and placed it next to its brothers and sisters.

It wasn't long before Little Red Riding Hood realised that she had strayed far from the path she usually took with her pony. Although the path was unfamiliar and the forest was very dark, Little Red Riding Hood wasn't afraid. She loved the forest and all the creatures that lived there. She knew she would be able to find the way to her grandmother's house eventually, so she skipped along, singing to herself and feeling very happy.

As Little Red Riding Hood went further into the forest, she started to feel very hungry. She remembered the fruitcake her mother had baked that was in the basket she carried, so she decided to stop for a while to eat a piece. “I’m sure grandmother won’t mind if I just try a little bit,” she said to herself as she sat down on the trunk of a fallen tree and unwrapped the cake from its clean white cloth.

Suddenly, there was the sound of a twig snapping and a rustling noise came from within the bushes. Little Red Riding Hood heard someone behind her clear his throat and say, “Hello, little girl. Are you lost? What are you doing eating cake all alone in the middle of this deep, dark forest?”

Little Red Riding Hood remembered that her mother had told her never to speak to strangers, but it didn’t seem polite to say nothing. Peering around her, she replied, “I’m off to visit my grandmother, to take her some good things to eat, because she is very old and lives all alone.”

Little Red Riding Hood didn't know that she was actually talking to a big bad wolf. He was hiding behind a tree and pretending to be nice, but really he was very wicked and only wanted to know where Little Red Riding Hood was going so that he could gobble her up. The wolf was very, very hungry. There was only one thing in the world he liked to eat more than cake, and that was little girls. The wolf was also very sly and cunning. He knew that if he pounced right now, the little girl would scream and scream, but if he was patient, he would be able to eat Little Red Riding Hood *and* her grandmother for his lunch!

"How kind of you to look after your grandmother so well," said the wolf in his most charming voice. "Where does she live?"

Little Red Riding Hood, who had completely forgotten that she shouldn't talk to strangers, replied, "She lives in the gamekeeper's cottage. You see, my grandfather was the gamekeeper, but he died a long time ago and now my grandmother is all alone..."

Before she had time to finish her story, Little Red Riding Hood heard a rustling from the bushes and realised that the stranger had gone. She peered into the darkness, but there was nothing to be seen – only a funny smell lingered in the air.

Little Red Riding Hood packed up her basket and set off once more through the deep, dark forest to her grandmother's house. As she approached the cottage, she stopped to pick her grandmother a beautiful big bunch of the brightest yellow flowers she could find. Meanwhile, the big bad wolf had hurried on ahead, slinking through the undergrowth to get to the gamekeeper's cottage first.

When the wolf arrived at the cottage, he knocked on the door.

"Who's there? called the quavery voice of a very old lady.

"It's Little Red Riding Hood," the big bad wolf replied in a high voice. "I've come to see my darling grandmother." He smiled a bad wolfish smile and licked his chops at the thought of the big meal ahead. "How lovely, my dear, but I'm taking my afternoon nap at the moment," said the grandmother, "so stand on your tippy-toes to lift the latch and come right on in."

The big bad wolf lifted the latch, the door creaked open and he was inside the cottage. "Come through to my bedroom, my dear," called the grandmother. The big bad wolf did as he was told, and when he saw the shape of the plump little grandmother under the blankets, his bright eyes flashed and his sharp yellow teeth glistened with moisture.

Before she could utter one squeak of surprise, the big bad wolf gobbled up the old lady in one gulp. Then he picked up the grandmother's frilly nightcap and pulled it on his furry head, he wrapped himself in her shawl, then he put the grandmother's glasses on his snout and tucked himself up in her bed.

The big bad wolf didn't have to wait long before there was a knock at the door. "Who's there?" he asked in the voice of a very old lady.

"It's me," replied Little Red Riding Hood, "I've come to see my darling grandmother."

The big bad wolf rubbed his paws together in anticipation. "Oh, how lovely, my dear, but I'm taking an afternoon rest at the moment," he quavered, "so stand on your tippy-toes to lift the latch and come right on in."

Little Red Riding Hood did as she was told and pushed open the creaky door.

There was a funny smell in the house and things didn't seem to be quite as they ought. Little Red Riding Hood couldn't say exactly what was wrong, except there was a tingling on the top of her head and her skin felt cold and shivery.

"Are you alright, Grandmother?" called Little Red Riding Hood anxiously. "I've brought you a delicious fruitcake baked fresh this morning."

"Then come into the bedroom, my dear, because I'm very, very hungry," came the quavery reply.

Little Red Riding Hood put her head around the bedroom door. It was dark in there because the shutters at the window were closed and the big heavy curtains around the four-poster bed were half-drawn. There was a fire in the grate and the old lady seemed to be knitting by candlelight.

"Come closer, my dear," came a quavery voice.

Little Red Riding Hood walked cautiously towards the bed and although it was dark, she got quite a shock. The knitting needles that flashed to and fro were gripped by two large hairy paws!

Little Red Riding Hood knew it was rude to point, but she couldn't help it. "Grandmother," she blurted out, "what big hairy hands you've got!"

"All the better to hug you with, my dear," said the big bad wolf in a quavery voice. "Come a little closer."

As Little Red Riding Hood took another step forward, she suddenly noticed that there were two furry ears poking from her grandmother's frilly nightcap. Although she'd been taught not to stare, Little Red Riding Hood couldn't help it. "Grandmother," she exclaimed, "what big furry ears you've got!"

The big bad wolf pulled the nightcap further down with his paws to hide his ears.

"All the better to hear you with, my dear," he replied. "Come a little closer, Little Red Riding Hood."

Little Red Riding Hood cautiously stepped closer still. In the flickering candlelight she noticed a pair of gleaming yellow eyes staring at her from under the purple nightcap.

Although she knew it was rude to comment, Little Red Riding Hood couldn't help it. "Grandmother," she cried out in astonishment, "what big yellow eyes you have!"

"All the better to see you with, my dear," said the wolf in a quavery voice. "Come a little closer."

Little Red Riding Hood stepped right up to the bed and saw two rows of jagged yellow teeth as sharp as knives. Now she was really alarmed. A tingle ran all the way down her spine as she squealed, "Grandmother, what enormous teeth you have!"

In a flash, the big bad wolf leaped out of bed, shouting, "All the better to eat you with, my dear!" Revealing himself as the wolf, his voice was not at all quavery, but rough and gruff and full of menace. Terrified, Little Red Riding Hood screamed as loud as she could and swung her basket at the wolf's nose. The basket hit the wolf, and the cake, the flowers, the butter and the eggs went flying through the air. Surprised at being hit by a little girl, the big bad wolf slipped in the mess and fell heavily to the floor in a heap!

At the very same moment, there was a loud knock on the door. Not waiting for a reply, the latch was lifted, the door burst open and Little Red Riding Hood's father, the woodcutter, stood in the doorway holding his sharp woodman's axe firmly in his hand.

Little Red Riding Hood ran to her father and he lifted her up into his strong arms. "The big bad wolf wanted to eat me!" she cried. Her father hugged her tight and wiped her tears away as she told him the whole dreadful story.

"You know you should never speak to strangers," he said gently, "even when they are friendly and polite."

Suddenly, Little Red Riding Hood clutched her father's arm and gasped. "The big bad wolf was dressed up in Grandmother's clothes," she cried, "but where is my darling grandmother now?" Little Red Riding Hood grabbed her father's hand and pulled him towards the rug where the big bad wolf lay unconscious. As they stared at the wolf, something very strange happened – his big, hairy, round tummy moved!

The woodcutter took his knife and very carefully slit open the wolf's tummy. Out popped Little Red Riding Hood's grandmother! "He swallowed me in one gulp!" she said, brushing herself down, "but thankfully I'm none the worse for wear."

The three of them were thrilled to be reunited after their terrible adventure. While the grandmother made tea, Little Red Riding Hood cut some cake, which had survived being thrown at the wolf, and her father quickly sewed up the wolf's tummy with some twine and rolled him out of the door.

"Good riddance, big bad wolf," he said, shutting the door firmly behind him.

Several hours later, the big bad wolf woke up with a terrible headache and a swollen tummy. "Ouch," he said to himself. "I'll never eat another old lady again. I'll never, never, ever try to trick another little girl. Little Red Riding Hood was far too clever for me." He held his tummy with one paw and his head with the other paw and slunk off into the forest, never to be seen again.

Little Red Riding Hood, her family and all the creatures of the forest lived happily ever after, safe in the knowledge that the big bad wolf had learned his lesson.

THE END

The Pied Piper of Hamelin

Once upon a time,

the town of Hamelin in Germany

had a terrible problem, which was a shame because the town itself was very beautiful. It had cobbled streets, old-fashioned houses with little windows and tall wooden beams and a pretty market square, outside the town hall, full of trees and flowers. The town also stood beside a fast-flowing river, the River Weser, which wound into the distance like a gigantic sparkling snake.

The problem with Hamelin was the rats! The place was full of them. They ran around everywhere – black rats, brown rats, grey rats, white rats and even rats with brown and black patches on their bodies. They came in all shapes and sizes. Some were baby rats with high-pitched squeaks. Others were hungry grown-up rats who bit anything that came near them. There were even elderly rats, as big as footballs, who had grown fat on eating everything they could find. Nothing was safe from these rodents.

They gnawed their way through walls, or tunnelled under floorboards, stealing food and ruining clothes and furniture. It was not unusual to find a huge rat sleeping in your shoe when you came to put it on!

As you would expect, the people of the town did everything they possibly could to get rid of these rats. They tried putting down traps. They tried putting down poison. They tried using fierce little terrier dogs and hunting cats that had not been fed for a week to make them extra hungry. Nothing seemed to work. The next day, the rats were always back in even greater numbers than before. In the end, the good folk of Hamelin gave up. It looked as if they would just have to get used to their unpleasant and unwelcome visitors. The rats were here to stay!

One day, a strange figure arrived in the market square. He was tall and thin with twinkling green eyes that looked full of fun and mischief. He wore funny-looking, old-fashioned clothes. Two quarters of his top and one trouser leg were dark red; the other parts were bright yellow – a colourful style called 'pied' as worn by court jesters in ancient castles. He also carried a flute in his right hand. When asked his name, the newcomer replied,

"I'm known as the Pied Piper."

As if to show what his name meant, the stranger put his flute to his lips and began to play a tune. The beautiful melody floated through the air like a magic spell, making everyone stop what they were doing and come forward to listen to the music. Soon, the Pied Piper was surrounded by a big crowd, all listening to him with their eyes wide open, as if in a trance.

Then they began clapping and cheering when the musician broke into song, singing the words they all wanted to hear:

"Bow your heads or raise your hats," he chanted, "I'm the one who'll get rid of your rats!"

Inside the town hall, the mayor was conducting yet another meeting of the town council to discuss how to get rid of the rats. He was very annoyed by all the shouting and cheering outside. "What's going on?" he yelled. "There are some very important people in here, talking about a very serious problem. How can we think clearly with all that noise going on?"

Taking no notice of the red-faced mayor, the Pied Piper strode into the town hall and put his flute down on the table.

"Gentlemen," he said to the astonished town councillors. "I can clear your town of rats by sunset this evening, if you wish!"

"Rubbish!" they shouted back, accusing their visitor of being a fake or some kind of dangerous wizard.

"Enough!" cried the mayor, holding up his hand. "Leave this to me. I'm the most important person here, so you must trust in my judgement. Tell us, mysterious stranger, what will you charge to get rid of our rats?"

"A gold coin for every rat," replied the Pied Piper.

"That's outrageous!" shouted the councillors. "There are thousands of rats, so we'll have to pay thousands of coins!"

"That is my price," replied the Piper, calmly.

"We'll take it!" cried the mayor. "We promise we'll pay you a gold coin a head to get rid of the rats. Just be quiet, the rest of you. I'm the leader of this town and I've told you – trust in my judgement!"

That evening, the Pied Piper toured the streets, telling people to stay indoors whilst he was at work. "You may watch from your windows," he called, "but please do not come outside until I have finished."

As the sun began to set, he put his flute to his lips and began playing some more of his beautiful music. At first, nothing happened. Then, from underneath a market stall, a rat appeared. It was soon followed by two or three more, running out from behind a sack of corn. Before long, a steady stream of rats was pouring out of the houses, shops, cellars and barns, all drawn by the enchanting music of the Pied Piper's flute.

The rats gathered in a squealing, squirming crowd around the Piper's feet.

"This way, my beauties," he called, putting his flute to his lips again and skipping along in front of the rodents. He played a lively dance that made the rats follow him in a long, wriggling line. Out of the town he led them, through the countryside and down to the banks of the River Weser. As the sky turned red and yellow, matching his funny clothes, the Pied Piper played faster than ever, making the rats race towards the water.

SPLISH! SPLOSH! SPLASH! One after another, the creatures plunged into the river. Being excellent swimmers, they did not drown. They gathered together in the middle of the stream, like a floating black cloud, and were washed downstream by the powerful current. Eventually, they reached a distant bend in the river where they scrambled out and ran off into some empty hills where they could do nobody any harm. They were never seen again.

The following morning, the people of Hamelin woke up to a strange silence. There was no gnawing in the larder or scraping under the floorboards or squeaking and squealing in the loft. The rats were gone! Waving and cheering, families poured out of their houses and surrounded the inn where the Pied Piper was staying. Then, like a conquering hero after a war, they carried him shoulder-high to the town hall to see the mayor once more.

The mayor's speech of thanks went on for half an hour. In the end, the Pied Piper interrupted him.

"When are you going to pay me?" he asked, bluntly.

"Er… um… I was just coming to that," said the mayor, shifting the big gold chain that hung around his neck. "How much do we owe you?"

"I counted ten thousand rats going into the river," replied the Pied Piper, "which means you owe me ten thousand gold coins."

"That's a coin a head, as we agreed?" asked the mayor.

"Correct!" replied the Piper.

"So where are the heads?" asked the mayor, barely able to hide the smirk on his face. "You say you're expecting a coin a head, so where are these heads? Let's see them!"

Of course, the mayor knew full well that the Pied Piper did not have any rats' heads. The phrase 'a coin a head' meant a piece of gold for every rat, but the mayor was pretending it meant exactly what it said. This was a cunning way to avoid handing over any money. As the Pied Piper realised he had been tricked, his face turned as black as thunder.

"Pay me my ten thousand gold coins!" he shouted.

"Certainly not!" cried the mayor, who was now being clapped and cheered by all the other councillors who realised they would not have to part with any of their precious money. "You have not kept your part of the agreement, so we don't have to keep ours. We will, however, give you fifty gold coins for your trouble."

The mayor held out the small bag of coins, but the Pied Piper brushed it aside .

"You shall still pay me," he hissed, going up close to the mayor's face and looking him straight in the eye, "but this time it won't be in money!"

The mayor just laughed and the councillors booed and hissed as the furious musician stormed out of the room.

"There," chuckled the mayor, proudly, "we've got rid of our rats without spending a single gold coin! I told you to trust in my judgement, didn't I?"

The following day was a Sunday. The custom in Hamelin in those days was for the adults to go to church in the morning, leaving the younger children to do the housework and the older ones to prepare lunch for when their parents returned. Normally, this meal was already half-eaten by rats. So, on this particular day, all the adults were really looking forward to coming home to a clean house and a lovely, peaceful meal.

The mayor was amongst the throng of people leaving their houses that morning.

"Make sure the vegetables are properly cooked," he called to his teenage daughter who stood waving goodbye to him on the doorstep. The mayor was particularly proud today. News of his brilliant trick had reached every citizen in the whole town of Hamelin. Realising their taxes would not have to go up to pay the Piper's fee, they had voted him their leader for life.

When all the adults had gone into the church, the Pied Piper stepped out onto the streets and put his flute to his lips once more. Never had he played such sweet music! The beautiful notes floated in through the open windows, reaching the ears of the children. Immediately, they stopped cleaning and cooking and hurried out of their houses, dancing and singing.

Before long, the market square contained every single child in the town, all under the spell of the haunting magic music. Slowly, the Piper started to lead the youngsters out into the country. This time, he did not head for the river. Instead, he went in the opposite direction and skipped through the lush meadows, heading for a distant mountain. The children followed in a long line, just like the rats, not knowing or even caring where they were going.

At twelve o'clock, when the church service was over, the people of Hamelin returned to their houses with puzzled looks on their faces. There were no clean floors or stairs to greet them, nor was there a delicious smell of Sunday lunch coming from the kitchens. Everywhere was silent and deserted.

"Where are our children?" they cried in alarm.

The trail of footprints leading from the town square showed which way the children had gone. Led by the mayor, the adults ran after the trail, wailing and screaming as they began to realise what had happened. They caught sight of the Pied Piper just as he reached the mountain with their children. Suddenly, two hidden doors in the mountainside swung open, revealing a huge room inside. Still playing his entrancing tunes, the Piper danced inside, followed by all the youngsters. CLANG! CLANG! The giant doors slammed shut, trapping the children within.

Yelling with panic, the adults fetched sticks and crowbars in the hope of prising open the doors.

"There are no gaps or cracks!" they cried. "This must be a magic mountain and the Pied Piper must be an evil magician! He has taken our children away from us and we'll never see them again."

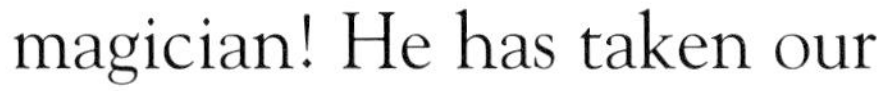

As if to make matters worse, the sound of the flute and the happy laughter of the children could be heard coming from inside the mountain.

For many days and nights, the good people of Hamelin waited in vain for their children's return. In the end, they realised their youngsters would stay inside the mountain for ever... unless the Pied Piper was paid. They hurried to their houses and emptied their money boxes, then they rushed to their banks and took all the money from their accounts. Finally, the people of Hamelin met outside the town hall and poured all their money into a huge pile.

When the mayor had counted exactly ten thousand gold coins, the money was put into bags and loaded onto a horse-drawn cart. The mayor himself drove the cart to the mountain, followed by a throng of anxious parents.

The Pied Piper was already waiting for them, standing alone in front of the doors with his hands on his hips.

"How do we know we can trust you?" called the mayor. "If we give you this money, how do we know you will give our children back?"

"I promise to release your children," answered the Pied Piper. "Unlike you, I am an honest man. I would never go back on my word – like you did!"

The watching crowd of parents gasped and began to whisper to one another. They had not been told that the mayor was to blame for the loss of their children. How could he and the councillors have been so selfish! They vowed to choose a new mayor as soon as they possibly could.

The waiting was agonising as the Piper opened every bag and counted every coin. When he was satisfied that he had been paid in full, he jumped onto the cart and drove off without another word. As he disappeared into the distance, the gigantic doors swung open and out rushed the children, straight into their parents' arms.

The young people of Hamelin had no idea what had happened or where they had been. Most of them thought they had been dreaming. Only the mayor's daughter remembered a fragment of a beautiful tune that made her want to dance just by thinking about it. Humming it quietly to herself, she waved goodbye to the Pied Piper who was now just a tiny speck going over the horizon.

THE END

Hansel and Gretel

Once upon a time, there lived a poor woodcutter named Jan and his two children Hansel and Gretel. Hansel was a brave and handsome boy with a mop of golden curls just like his father. His sister Gretel, with her long dark hair and deep brown eyes, had been blessed with the beauty of their mother.

The woodcutter's wife had died when the children were very young. Every time Jan gazed upon his daughter, he felt sad as he remembered his dear wife. Although Jan deeply missed Hansel and Gretel's mother, he was very lonely and longed for the company of a new wife.

Before long, the woodcutter decided to marry a widow from the village. She was a fearful woman with a fiery temper, but Jan hoped that she would make a good wife and mother.

She did not! The stepmother was cruel and unkind to Hansel and Gretel and very soon the children realised that she would never love them as their real mother had done.

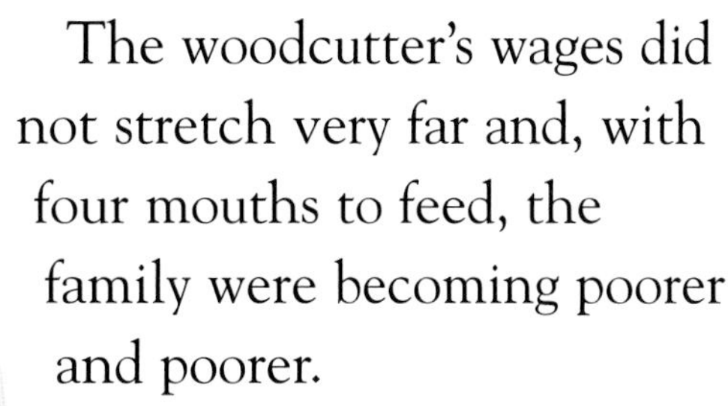

The woodcutter's wages did not stretch very far and, with four mouths to feed, the family were becoming poorer and poorer.

One night, Hansel and Gretel overheard their father and stepmother talking. Their stepmother had a wicked plan to make the family's money last longer. "Tomorrow you must take Hansel and Gretel deep into the forest, then leave them alone while you pretend to search for firewood," she said. "With those greedy children out of the way, there will be far more food for us." Jan tried to argue with his wife, but she insisted that he should carry out the evil scheme.

Hansel and Gretel couldn't believe their ears. How could their father betray them? The children, however, were a brave and clever pair and soon devised a plan of their own. They crept downstairs and searched the garden for as many small pebbles as they could find. Having filled their pockets with the tiny stones, they returned to bed and waited anxiously until morning.

It was with a heavy heart that Jan led his two children into the forest the following day. Just as his wife had instructed, he told Hansel and Gretel to wait in a clearing whilst he collected logs for the fire. He then made his way home, leaving the children alone in the forest.

Unbeknown to their father, Hansel and Gretel had left a trail of pebbles from the cottage to the forest as they walked behind him. Once they realised their father really wasn't coming back for them, they followed the path of pebbles all the way home.

"Thank goodness you're safe," cried their father when he saw Hansel and Gretel at the door. He was pleased that the plan had failed. His wife, on the other hand, was furious. She locked Hansel and Gretel in their bedroom without any supper.

Later that night, the children overheard the adults talking again. "Tomorrow, you must take Hansel and Gretel to the deepest, darkest part of the forest," said the stepmother, "and make sure that they never find their way back again."

Jan tried to protest. "How can you expect me to leave my own children in the forest to die?" he pleaded. The woodcutter's new wife was a cruel and heartless woman. "We can't afford to keep the children," she argued. "If we do, we are all doomed to die of starvation." Once again, the woodcutter reluctantly agreed to the plan.

The next day, Hansel and Gretel obediently followed their father into the forest. Since they had been locked in their room the night before, they had not been able to collect any pebbles to drop on the path. Suddenly, Hansel had an idea. Instead of eating the crust of bread his father had given him, he began breaking it into crumbs and scattering it behind him as he walked. Gretel soon realised what her brother was doing and when Hansel had used up all of his bread, she continued the trail with her own piece.

When the time came for Jan to leave his children, he hugged them both with tears in his eyes. "Stay here and play whilst I go and collect logs," he said. "I shall return for you in two hours." With that, he walked off into the trees.

Hansel and Gretel were not down-hearted. They had found their way back home before and with the help of their secret trail, they were sure they could do so once again. When they looked for their breadcrumb trail, however, the children got a nasty surprise. It had completely disappeared! The hungry woodland birds had eaten every morsel of white crust – it seemed that Hansel and Gretel really were lost forever.

The children felt desperately sad and all alone. They sat down under a huge oak tree, huddled up close together and began to cry. Just then, Gretel noticed a beautiful bird with bright blue feathers and shining silver wings. She dried her eyes and nudged her brother.

"Hansel, look at that wonderful bird!" she exclaimed. "It seems to be calling to us." Sure enough, the bird was whistling a haunting tune and encouraging the children to follow it through the forest.

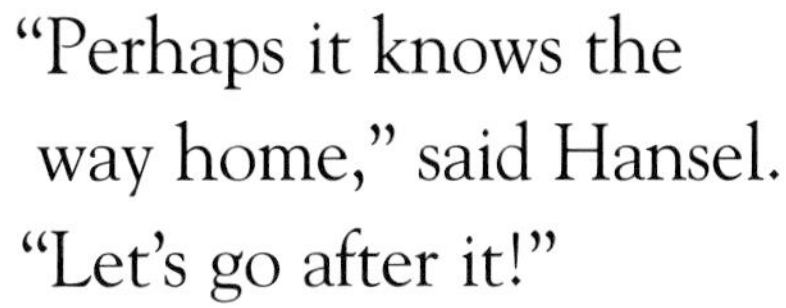

"Perhaps it knows the way home," said Hansel. "Let's go after it!"

The brother and sister held hands and followed the bird as it flitted from tree to tree. They walked for hours and became tired, thirsty and incredibly hungry. Just when they thought they could walk no further, the silver-winged bird led them to a clearing.

Hansel and Gretel could hardly believe their eyes – they were faced by a beautiful and magical sight. In the clearing stood a cottage that was made entirely of cake and candy. Desperate for food, they ran up to the cottage and began licking the bricks, breaking off lumps of window ledge and nibbling the roof tiles.

Suddenly, an old woman appeared at the door. "You poor children," she said kindly, "you must be famished. Come inside and I'll prepare you a proper meal."

The children timidly followed the woman into the candy cottage. True to her word, the sweet old lady provided Hansel and Gretel with a hearty supper of hot chicken soup and freshly baked bread. Then she offered them a bed for the night, which the tired children gratefully accepted.

The next morning, Hansel and Gretel felt happy and refreshed. They were sure that the mysterious and magical keeper of the candy cottage would help them find their way back through the forest to their father's house. The woman who came to their room to wake them, however, was not the kindly, grey-haired old lady they had met the night before. In her place stood a hideous old witch with gnarled features and an evil glint in her eye.

The witch cackled hysterically, threw an apron at Gretel and told her to go down to the kitchen. Then she grabbed Hansel by the ear and dragged him downstairs too.

Gretel was told to get to work peeling potatoes, whilst her brother was thrown into a cage in the corner of the room. "This is what happens to greedy little children who come nosing around my cottage," screeched the old hag. She locked the door of the cage and hung the key on a hook high up on the kitchen wall.

Hansel and Gretel were shocked by the old woman's horrible transformation, but they were a quick-witted pair and knew that they could escape from the evil witch if only they could think of a way to distract her.

As Gretel took a closer look around the cottage, it became clear that she and her brother weren't the first unfortunate souls to stumble across the old witch's lair. Clothes, hats, purses and jewels belonging to the witch's previous victims were to be seen stashed under chairs, on shelves and in cupboards.

"If we could return home with all this money and jewellery, our worries would be over," thought Gretel.

The witch was an especially evil old woman. Not only did she steal the belongings of anyone who called at her cottage, but she took great delight in tempting the travellers inside, then boiling them up in her cauldron and eating them for her supper! Tender young boys were her particular favourite and she was looking forward to fattening up poor Hansel and then picking his bones clean with her disgusting yellow teeth. The witch was also a lazy old hag, so it was left to Gretel to cook all the meals and clean the cottage every day.

The young girl had strict instructions to feed her brother well with thick broths, plenty of potatoes and lots of buttery cakes in order to plump him up ready for the pot.

Every morning, the witch would tell Hansel to poke his finger through the bars of the cage so that she could feel whether he was any fatter.

Having spent years eating the simple meals provided by his poor father, Hansel welcomed Gretel's daily diet of rich food. Try as he might, he just couldn't help devouring the delicious meals served up by his sister. Soon the boy's pale cheeks had become plump and rosy and the belt on his tattered trousers had become a little tighter. The children knew that if Hansel's fingers became too fat, the witch would eat him.

One day, whilst she was preparing soup, Gretel looked down at the chicken bones on the table. "Hansel," she whispered, "quickly take this bone and hide it in your pocket. When the witch asks to feel your finger, simply poke the bone through the bars of the cage instead. Her eyesight is so bad, she'll never notice the difference."

For a while, the plan seemed to work. Everyday, the witch inspected Hansel's bony finger and everyday she declared that he was still too skinny to be eaten. After three weeks of waiting, the witch finally lost her patience. "That's it," she cried, "I'm tired of waiting for you to get fatter. Tonight I will feast on roast leg of boy!" Then the witch ordered Gretel to heat up the huge oven.

Hansel and Gretel had been living in the cottage for quite a while. By now they knew that, as well as being cruel, lazy and very short-sighted, the witch was also rather stupid. The brother and sister were sure that they could out-wit the old woman one more time. As the day wore on, the witch became increasingly excited about her evening meal. She flitted madly around the kitchen, gathering together ingredients and ordering Gretel to do this and to do that.

The witch was particularly worried about the temperature of the oven and kept asking Gretel to open the cast iron door to check that the stove was still alight.

"Stick your head inside girl," ordered the witch, "and make sure that the flame is still flickering." Hansel and Gretel looked at each other and smiled – they both knew that this could be the route to their escape.

"I'm afraid I can't reach to the back of the oven," replied Gretel sweetly, "could you help me please?" By now the witch was desperate for her dinner. She pushed Gretel aside angrily and grabbed the handle of the oven door.

"You stupid child," she screeched, "do I have to do everything myself?"

The witch opened the oven and poked her revolting, wrinkled head inside.

At that moment, Gretel leapt into action.

Quick as a flash, she pushed the witch headfirst into the hot oven. Then, with the evil old woman's screams ringing in her ears, the young girl slammed the heavy door shut. With the witch out of the way, Gretel could free her brother from his cage at last. She grabbed a kitchen chair and climbed up to get the key from the hook.

"Well done, Gretel," said Hansel with a smile. "I couldn't have done any better myself."

The children were keen to escape from the candy cottage as soon as possible, but they also knew that the witch's ill-gotten riches would come in very useful. They stuffed their pockets with as much money and jewellery as they could before leaving the witch's house for ever.

"We may have escaped from the evil witch, but we still have to find our way home," Hansel reminded Gretel as they ran into the forest. Just then, the brother and sister heard a distant yet familiar voice calling their names.

"Hansel, Gretel, where are you?" It was their father, Jan. As soon as he left his children in the forest, he had regretted his terrible actions and had spent every day since searching the forest for Hansel and Gretel. His new wife, meanwhile, had grown tired of her husband's desperate attempts and was angry that he was earning even less money than before. She had stolen what little food the woodcutter had and returned to the village.

"I've found you at last," cried Jan when he saw his beautiful children running through the forest towards him. He clasped Hansel and Gretel to his chest and promised that he would never betray them again. "I would rather be a poor woodcutter than lose my dear Hansel and Gretel," he said.

"Father," cried Hansel, "we need never be poor again!" The two smiling children revealed their hoard of money and beautiful jewels. Jan was amazed and overjoyed. Not only had he found his children but, thanks to Hansel and Gretel, the family's money worries were at an end. With that, Jan and his two children made their way home to the woodcutter's little cottage where they lived happily ever after.

THE END

The Emperor's New Clothes

Once upon a time, there was an emperor who was very vain. This rich and powerful ruler spent no time at all in the council chamber, talking with his government ministers about how to run the country. Instead, he spent all his time in his bedroom, trying on different sets of clothes and admiring himself in the full-length mirror. In fact, whenever he passed a mirror on the palace walls, he would stop to check his appearance!

Every morning, the emperor put on a brand new outfit. An hour later, after breakfast, he would be tired of this first outfit and change into a second one. By lunch time, he had usually worn two or three more completely different sets of clothes… and so on, every couple of hours, until the end of each day. By the time the emperor went to bed at night, his poor servants had to sort out a huge mountain of clothes tossed into a corner of the royal bedroom.

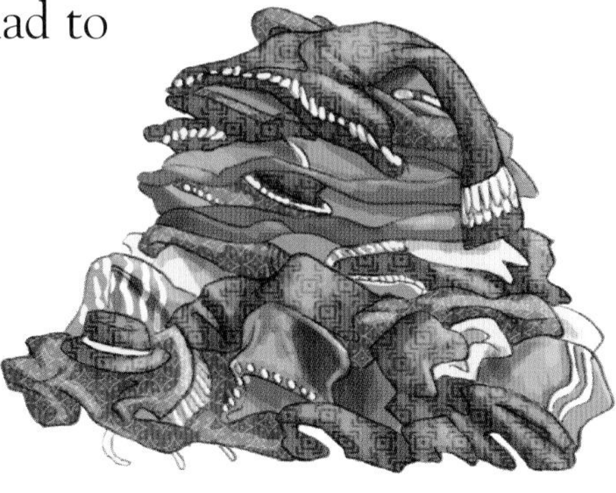

One day, a pair of crooks arrived in town. They had heard how vain the Emperor was and decided to trick him out of lots of money.

"We'll pretend to be weavers," said the first crook.

"Yeah," chuckled the second. "We'll sell his Highness some very special cloth."

At this time, weaving was a long and difficult job. It needed lots of skill if the cloth was to be suitable to make fashionable clothes and the emperor was an impatient man. When the two crooks called at the palace, the emperor was delighted.

"Come in, come in!" he cried. "I can't wait to see samples of your work."

The cunning tricksters showed the emperor some ordinary cloth, just the same as the material used to make the clothes he was wearing. The emperor certainly wasn't very interested in that.

Then the crooks went on to explain that they could make a cloth that was magic, but very expensive.

"It's extremely special, Your Majesty," explained the first crook.

"That's right," added the second crook. "Not only is the pattern unquestionably exquisite, but the cloth is so thin and fine, it's invisible to anyone who is not fit for office or unpardonably stupid."

Naturally, the emperor was intrigued.

"If what you say is true," he cried, excitedly, "the clothes that are made from this special cloth will make me look amazing! Bring your loom to the palace and start work right away. I will give you as much money as you want to finish the job."

The crooks looked at each other and winked. The emperor had fallen for their cunning plan and money and riches would soon be theirs!

Next day, the rattle and hum of the weaving loom could be heard all around the emperor's palace. The crooks performed a clever act in which they pretended to be weaving invisible thread into invisible cloth when, in fact, they weren't weaving anything at all! Their loom was completely empty!

Pacing around his bedroom, the emperor could hardly wait to see the special cloth that he had paid so much money for. The more he paced, the more nervous he became. What if he couldn't see the cloth? He didn't think he was stupid or unfit for his job, but... "I'd better send someone to have a look at it for me," he muttered to himself, "just in case."

The emperor called for the most important official in the government, the prime minister, and sent him to inspect the new material.

"Remember," he called, as the prime minister set off down the corridor, "you won't be able to see this amazing creation if you're not very clever or can't do your job properly."

The prime minister entered the room where the two men were working. Since there was nothing there, the poor prime minister couldn't see the wonderful magic cloth at all!

Noticing the puzzled look on the prime minister's face, the first crook asked, "What's the matter? Don't you like the colour of this cloth?"

The prime minister didn't want to appear stupid, so he replied, "No! It's a lovely colour! Beautiful bright red!"

Then the second crook asked, "And the pattern? What do you think about that?"

"It's... er... most unusual," stammered the prime minister, who didn't want the crooks to think he was unable to do his job as well. "I particularly like those golden circles. Very pretty indeed!"

With that, the puzzled man hurried back to the emperor where he reported that the magic cloth was the most beautiful colour and had the most amazing pattern of any cloth he had seen in his life!

The emperor was delighted and relieved – he trusted his loyal and honest prime minister.

By now, it was dinner time. The two crooks were led to a beautiful suite of rooms where they were given the finest food and the softest beds in the land.

The next morning, the emperor realised he had been dreaming about his luxury cloth. He imagined its vibrant colours and beautiful patterns, but he still felt it was too early to see it for himself.

The emperor decided to send his deputy prime minister, the second most important official in the government, to inspect the weavers' work. This man was also reminded that the cloth would appear invisible if he was stupid or unfit to do his job.

The deputy prime minister scratched his head in bewilderment when the two men showed him the cloth.

"Don't you like the zigzag pattern?" asked the first crook.

"And what about the colour?" added the second.

"Incredible!" exclaimed the deputy prime minister, who wanted the emperor to know he was both clever and good at his job. "I'll go and tell the Emperor at once!"

On hearing the deputy prime minister's report, the emperor could wait no longer. He rushed to the weaving room, burst through the doors… and stopped. He was faced by a completely empty loom and there was no new cloth in sight!

The emperor remembered what he had told the prime minister and the deputy prime minister. 'If they can see the cloth,' he thought to himself, 'then I'd better pretend I can see it too. I must appear clever and fit to be emperor – after all, it's the most important job in the land.'

The emperor wandered around the loom, pretending he could see the new cloth. He praised the skill of the weavers and told them he was stunned by the cloth's wonderful colours and amazing patterns.

"Now kindly take my measurements," he said, holding out his arms. "I want a suit made from this wonderful material to be ready by tomorrow morning. I shall wear it to the grand procession I'm planning to make around the city. I can't wait for people to see me in this beautiful new cloth."

The two men busied themselves with tape measures, turning the emperor around and around and asking him to pose in every position they could think of.

That night, the weavers were seen cutting the imaginary cloth and sewing pieces together that didn't exist. They worked through the night until the candles burned low. When they heard the first cockerel crow at the break of dawn, the crooks flopped onto their luxury beds, pretending to be exhausted by their hard night's work. In fact, they were both laughing to themselves at the way in which they had managed to fool everybody – especially the most important person in all the land!

The next morning, the emperor woke up early, excited about the delivery of his new suit of clothes. There was a knock at the door and in strode the first so-called weaver. His hands were outstretched as if he was carrying something.

"Here's your splendid new jacket, Sire," he said, smiling.

"And here are your wonderful new trousers," said the second weaver, following behind. "Both are so light and delicate, you won't even know you're wearing them!"

The emperor was so keen to feel this special material against his skin that he took off his dressing gown and his pyjamas immediately. He stood before the mirror, completely naked, waiting to be dressed in his new suit. The two men stood either side of the emperor, handing him the imaginary clothes and pretending to adjust them here and there for a perfect fit.

The finishing touch was an imaginary feather hat that was carefully placed on the emperor's head.

"How do I look?" asked the emperor, giving a twirl in front of his full-length mirror.

"Dazzling!" lied the first crook.

"Magnificent!" lied the second.

The Emperor beamed from ear to ear with pleasure.

"Here's another fifty gold pieces," he said, handing over a bulging bag of coins. "A token of my thanks for doing such an excellent job!"

Laughing and giggling together, the two tricksters hurried away from the palace, carrying the bags full of gold that the foolish emperor had given them.

Meanwhile, the emperor made the final preparations for his grand procession.

The emperor went to find the prime minister in order to confirm the details of the grand procession.

"I shall walk through the streets of the city accompanied by four footmen carrying a canopy over my head," he said. "It might rain and I can't afford to get this priceless new suit wet."

The prime minister was speechless. The emperor stood before him, naked and shivering.

"Are you all right, Sire?" asked the prime minister.

"Of course I'm all right!" snapped the emperor. "It's just that these new clothes of mine are so light and delicate, they're not very warm for this time of year."

"Very good, Sire," replied the prime minister and went about his duties with a worried look on his face.

At twelve noon, a royal proclamation was read out to the people of the city. The town criers told everyone that the emperor was wearing special clothes that could only be seen by people who were clever and good at their jobs. Stupid people, or those who were no good at their work, would not be able to see them.

Amidst a deafening fanfare of trumpets, the great man himself appeared in the streets with four footmen holding a canopy over his head. A huge gasp went up from the crowd. The emperor thought it was because his new clothes were so breathtakingly beautiful. In fact, it was because he was not wearing anything at all!

Just like the prime minister and the deputy prime minister had been afraid to speak the truth, the people of the town did not wish to appear dim-witted or no good at their jobs. They clapped and cheered and shouted their praises of the emperor's new clothes.

"We're so lucky to have such a modern emperor!" called the baker.

"He's so fashionable!" cried the shoemaker.

"Hurray for the emperor!" shouted everyone together.

There was one little boy in the crowd who hadn't heard the announcement made by the town criers. He didn't know anything about the special cloth and how only people who were clever and good at their jobs were able to see it. He was the only one who said what he really saw.

"Look, mummy," he cried, tugging at his mother's sleeve and pointing. "The emperor's got no clothes on!"

Suddenly, the cheering stopped. The people in the crowd turned to one another and asked one another if it could be true. Was the emperor really parading the streets naked? People realised that the little boy was telling the truth and that they had been fooled.

One by one, people started to laugh and point at the tubby white figure of the emperor in front of them.

"Fancy walking around the town in the nude!" the shoemaker chuckled.

"I've never heard such nonsense!" tittered the baker. "Special clothes… he's got nothing on!"

Soon everyone was laughing so much that tears started to roll down their faces. Even the footmen joined in, shaking with laughter so hard that they could hardly hold the canopy over their master's head.

Looking around him, the emperor realised that he had been tricked. Snatching down the canopy and wrapping it around his naked body, he hurried back to the palace.

With his face bright red with embarrassment, the emperor rushed to his bedroom and slammed the door. He knew the crooked weavers were gone, so he couldn't take out his anger on them. He turned it on himself instead.

"What a fool I've been!" he exclaimed, grabbing all his fine clothes and flinging them into a pile.

Then he went around the palace, getting rid of all the mirrors in which he had been so fond of admiring himself. His special suit of clothes had taught him a lesson.

"I'm never going to be vain again for as long as I live!" he vowed, "and from now on I'll only wear plain suits made from very ordinary material!"

THE END

Jack and the Beanstalk

Once upon a time, there was a widow who lived with her only son, Jack. This poor lady loved her boy very much, but he was lazy and selfish and wasted what little money they had on things for himself. In fact, it wasn't long before their savings had been completely used up. All they had left was one milk cow.

After a sleepless night, Jack's mother made a difficult decision. "You'll have to take the cow to market and sell her, Jack," she said. "Make sure you get a good price for her!"

On the way to the market, Jack met an old man.

"Hey! Look at these!" called the stranger, showing Jack a handful of large beans.

"What about them?" asked Jack. "They look pretty ordinary to me!"

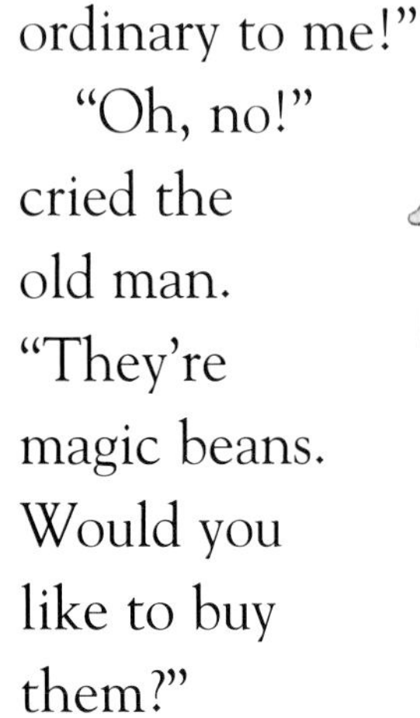

"Oh, no!" cried the old man. "They're magic beans. Would you like to buy them?"

Jack explained to the old man that he didn't have a penny to his name.

"What about the cow?" asked the stranger. "She must be worth a bit!"

"Of course!" exclaimed Jack. "I was on my way to market to sell her. I could swap her for your magic beans instead!"

When Jack got home, his mother was furious that he had swapped their cow for a handful of brown beans.

"You stupid boy!" she scolded. "Now we don't have any money at all. How are we going to live?"

"But these are magic beans, mum…" protested Jack.

"Nonsense!" shrieked his mother, snatching the beans out of his hand. She flung them as hard as she could out of the window.

"You've been tricked, Jack!" she shouted. "Those beans aren't magic. How could you have been so careless? Now we don't have any money to buy food and our cow has gone forever!"

That night, Jack went to bed feeling very miserable. He had no supper because the larder was empty and his mother was still very cross with him.

The following morning, Jack woke up expecting to see bright sunlight streaming through his window. Strangely, his room remained dark. Jack looked through the window and his jaw dropped in amazement. Outside, in the garden, one of the beans had grown into a gigantic beanstalk, reaching right up to the sky. Maybe the beans were magic after all!

"MUM!" yelled Jack, rushing outside. "Look at this!"

Jack had already started to climb the beanstalk, when his mother came outside to find out what he was shouting about.

"Jack!" she called, anxiously. "Jack, come down! The beanstalk might not be safe."

"It's as strong as a tree," Jack yelled back.

"But you don't know what you'll find up there!" shouted his mother.

Jack wasn't listening. He was already half-way up the beanstalk, climbing as fast as he could.

As Jack's head poked through the clouds, he found himself in a strange country. There was grass as far as the eye could see and empty, treeless hills rose in the distance. Then, turning around, Jack was startled to see a house – and not just any house. This house was enormous!

Jack walked up to the house and knocked boldly on the front door. A giant woman opened the door and glared down at him.

"Go away!" she hissed, urgently. "My husband will be back soon. He doesn't like little boys, especially human ones. He makes them his slaves!"

After his long, hard climb (and having gone to bed without any supper), Jack felt hungry and thirsty. He wasn't afraid of the giant and begged the giant's wife to let him in and give him something to eat and drink. In the end, she agreed.

Jack entered the huge house and looked around in amazement. All the rooms and the furniture were twenty times bigger than in his own home.

Jack had just finished eating and drinking when the THUD, THUD, THUD of approaching footsteps was heard outside.

"My husband's coming!" gasped the giant's wife. "Quick! Hide in the empty oven."

The very next moment, the door burst open and in strode the most enormous man that Jack had ever seen!

"Fee, fi, fo, fum!" he chanted, and his voice echoed around the room. "I can smell a human one!"

Jack thought he would be discovered, but the giant's wife covered for him.

"No, dear," she said. "You can smell this bacon I'm frying for your supper. Now sit down and make yourself comfortable. I've done you three hundred rashers as usual."

Peeping out from his hiding place, Jack watched the giant gobble up his huge supper in a few quick mouthfuls.

After supper, the woman put a small brown hen in front of her husband. Jack was worried the giant would eat the hen too! Instead, the giant began gently stroking the bird and cooing at her, like someone talking to a baby. Jack soon found out why. The giant's hen laid a golden egg. It rolled along the table, gleaming and sparkling in the light of the fire.

Jack quickly realised that this hen was the answer to all his problems. As soon as the giant dropped off to sleep and his wife was busy clearing up, the boy sneaked out of the oven, grabbed the hen and ran out of the house with it. He didn't stop running until he reached the top of the beanstalk. Then he clambered down as fast as he could, clutching the hen tightly under one arm.

Jack's mother was waiting at the bottom of the beanstalk.

"Where have you been?" she cried. "I've been so worried about you!"

"Sorry," replied Jack, "but look – I've brought you this." He put the little brown hen down in front of his mother.

"Well, at least we'll have some eggs to eat tonight," said his mother with a sigh.

"Oh, we'll have more than that!" chuckled Jack, and just at that moment, the hen laid another glittering golden egg!

By selling their solid gold eggs, Jack and his mother soon became wealthy. They bought a whole herd of cows, so they always had milk and cheese, and they bought some ordinary hens to give them proper fresh eggs. Their larder was always full and they wore fine clothes. In fact, they had all they wanted and should have lived happily ever after.

Jack, however, had enjoyed his thrilling adventure in the strange land above the clouds so much that he wanted to take another look. Life was now comfortable, but dull, and the beanstalk still stood invitingly outside the kitchen window. One day, Jack kissed his mother goodbye and scrambled up through the giant leaves in search of new excitement. He carried a false beard in his backpack so that he wouldn't be recognised by the giant's wife.

Jack jumped from the top of the beanstalk and looked around him. Everything seemed the same as before, so he put on the false beard and headed for the giant's house. The giant's wife opened the door and, at first, refused to let him in.

"A while ago," she said, "I let a human boy into the house and he stole my husband's special hen. Never a day goes by without him grumbling about it!"

Jack, however, pleaded with the woman until she changed her mind and let him in for some food and drink. By the time the giant's heavy footsteps were heard approaching, Jack was safely hidden in a kitchen cupboard.

"Fee, fi, fo, fum." roared the giant. "I smell another human one."

"No you don't, dear," said his wife, quickly. "You can smell the roast beef I'm cooking for your supper."

The giant sat down with a grunt and gobbled down fifty joints of beef, five hundred roast potatoes and the biggest apple pies Jack had ever seen!

"Wife!" yelled the giant when he had finished eating, "bring me my money! I want to count it again."

The giant's favourite pastime after supper, now that his magic hen had gone, was to tip out his bag of silver coins and run them through his hands, making them sparkle in the firelight. Jack's eyes nearly popped out of his head when he saw how many coins the giant had saved!

The giant's wife went up to bed, leaving her husband at the kitchen table. The giant carefully piled the coins into stacks, then counted each coin in every stack. Then he swept his enormous hand through the pile and started all over again. Just when Jack thought the giant would be awake all night, the giant poured the coins back into the bag.

The giant gave a satisfied grunt and fell fast asleep in his comfy armchair. As soon as Jack heard the giant snoring, he silently sneaked out of the cupboard and picked up the bag of silver coins. It was terribly heavy and the coins chinked together when the bag moved, but the giant was sound asleep and Jack managed to get his stolen treasure out of the house without being discovered.

Jack slithered down the beanstalk where his mother was waiting.

"Promise me you'll never go up that beanstalk again," she said. "We have enough money now to last us for the rest of our lives!"

Three whole years passed before Jack began to feel restless again. He and his mother now had everything they wanted. They slept in soft, comfy beds, they both owned fine horses on which they went riding, they even enjoyed a holiday in a castle by the sea… but it was still not enough for Jack. Every day, he looked at the beanstalk outside his bedroom window and wondered what fantastic adventure awaited him if he climbed it again.

One summer morning, with his mother tugging at his clothes and pleading with him not to go, Jack climbed the beanstalk for the third time. On this occasion, he did not need a disguise. He had grown quite a lot in three years and was now a tall and handsome young man.

"Please go away!" said the giant's wife, opening the door of the huge house in the land above the clouds. "I get into terrible trouble every time I let a human enter. My husband has already lost his best hen and his bag of precious silver!"

Jack needed to use all his powers of persuasion to make the enormous woman change her mind.

At last he succeeded and, following some refreshments, found himself hiding in the larder. THUD, THUD, THUD! The giant's heavy footsteps were heard coming into the kitchen.

"Fee, fi, fo, fum!" growled the giant, "I can smell a human one!"

"Don't be silly, dear," called his wife. "That's the smell of the lamb stew that I'm cooking for your supper."

Now you would eat stew from a plate, wouldn't you? Not this giant! He ate his stew from a bowl the size of a paddling pool, using a spoon the size of a grandfather clock and four hundred loaves of bread to wipe around the edges! When he had finished, the giant gave a burp that shook the house like an earthquake and then sat back, calling for his harp.

Jack watched in amazement as the giant's wife put a glittering gold harp beside her husband and it began to play beautiful music all by itself!

"That harp is all I need to finish my adventures with the giant," thought Jack, so he waited until the giant had been lulled to sleep by the enchanting music.

When Jack could hear the giant's snores and was sure that the giant's wife was out of the room, he leapt from his hiding place and grabbed the harp from the table. As he turned to run to the top of the beanstalk, to his horror, the harp seemed to come alive in his hands!

"Master, master!" called the magical instrument, sounding its strings all at once. "Help me, master! I'm being stolen by a horrible human!"

With a terrifying roar, the giant woke up and scrambled out of his chair. He raced after Jack and his beautiful harp.

At first, Jack thought he would get caught and be made into a slave for the rest of his life, but the giant was big and slow, and his tummy was very full of food.

Tucking the harp under his arm and running faster than he had ever run in his life, Jack raced across the stony ground towards the beanstalk, keeping just ahead of the giant.

Scrambling down the beanstalk, Jack gasped as he realised that the giant had started to follow after him. By the time the boy reached the ground, the huge figure was already nearly half-way down the beanstalk which was swaying under the weight.

"Mother, mother!" shouted Jack. "Fetch me the axe – as fast as you can!"

CHOP, CHOP, CHOP! Jack hacked away at the thick base of the beanstalk as fast as he could until there was an almighty CRASH. The massive beanstalk came tumbling to the ground.

Jack expected the giant to come tumbling down with the beanstalk, but with a roar of fury that echoed around the sky like thunder, the gigantic figure just managed to scramble back up to the top before he lost his grip.

Without the beanstalk there to tempt him, Jack never felt the need to go adventuring again. He married a beautiful girl, had two lovely children and looked after his mother as she grew older. Now he was a kind and thoughtful son, not the lazy and selfish one he had been before he climbed the beanstalk!

THE END

Tom Thumb

Merlin the magician was lost in the heart of a mysterious forest. He was travelling back home to King Arthur's mystical kingdom of Camelot, but had somehow lost his way. It was a dark and frosty night. A full moon cast a glow over the trees and, through the shadows, Merlin saw a light shining from a cottage in the distance.

Wrapping his long cloak around him for warmth, Merlin headed for the cottage and knocked on the door. A farmer and his wife welcomed him in. They took pity on the old man and offered him food and shelter for the night. He appeared so cold, tired and hungry, the couple didn't recognise him as King Arthur's great magician.

The farmer and his wife were good-hearted people, whose cottage was warm and comfortable, yet they both seemed so unhappy.

As Merlin ate his bowl of milk and coarse brown bread, he asked them why they were so sad.

"We are sad because we have no child," said the wife, trying not to cry. "If we had a son, even if he were no bigger than my husband's thumb, we would love him dearly."

The next day, Merlin bid the farmer and his wife thanks and farewell, and went to see his good friend, the queen of the fairies. When he told her of the kindness he had been shown, she agreed to help him repay the farmer and his wife. Both Merlin and the fairy queen were enchanted by the idea of a boy no bigger than a thumb, and so granted the farmer and his wife their wish. The couple were overjoyed that they now had a son and, true to their word, they loved him dearly.

The queen of the fairies kissed the little boy and named him Tom Thumb. She became his fairy godmother. In celebration, all the fairies made Tom Thumb a gift of some very special clothes.

Tom's shirt was spun from the threads of a spider's web,
His jacket and trousers were sewn from thistle down.
He wore bright red stockings of apple rind,
And an oak-leaf hat that he wore as a crown.
He had special shoes made of butter-polished leather,
Which were extremely hardwearing no
matter the weather.

Since Tom would grow no bigger, his clothes were made to last a very long time – after all, he would never outgrow them. Of course, his parents made sure that he had other things to wear, but his mother took special care of the clothes the fairies had given him. His favourite shirt spun from the spider's web was spectacular and his beautiful leather shoes fitted perfectly.

The world was a dangerous place for little Tom Thumb. For someone so small, he enjoyed great adventures and was always getting up to mischief.

Sometimes he'd get into trouble that wasn't really his fault – like the time he toppled head first into the pudding mix!

His mother had been stirring the mix in a bowl with a wooden spoon and Tom had tried to sneak a peek at the pudding because it smelled delicious. His mother was so busy stirring, she hadn't noticed him near the edge of the bowl. Unfortunately, he wobbled and toppled into the mix!

Tom began shouting to his mother, "Help me! Get me out!" Seeing the pudding mix moving before her eyes and thinking it was under the spell of witches, his mother was afraid and threw the bowl out of the kitchen window.

A beggar passing by couldn't believe his luck when he caught the pudding bowl still full of the delicious mixture. When he heard the pudding scream and shout, however, the beggar dropped the bowl to the ground and ran off in fear of being spellbound.

Realising what had happened, Tom's mother rushed outside, picked up her son from the mess of pudding mix and took him inside. She washed the pudding mix off him in a cup of soapy water.

Tom was unhurt after his adventure, but was quite upset. His mother dried him gently and put him to bed.

Tom's bed was made from part of a chestnut tree,
Carved by his father, it smelled like spring leaves.
The feather-down quilt had a colourful cover,
Lovingly sewn by Tom Thumb's mother.

The adventures didn't stop there, though! Tom once went with his mother to milk the brown cow. To keep Tom safe while she was busy, his mother sat him on a wisp of hay. When she wasn't looking, however, the cow took a mouthful of hay, including the wisp where Tom sat. Poor Tom ended up in the cow's mouth!

Trying to avoid the cow's teeth as she chewed on the hay, Tom began to shout, "Help, I'm in the brown cow's mouth. Get me out! Get me out!"

Tom's mother was alarmed… and so was the cow! The cow opened her mouth and out jumped Tom. He landed safely in his mother's apron.

Tom had another amazing adventure when he was working in the fields with his father. A raven flew overhead and spotted the boy. The raven swooped down and grabbed Tom Thumb's jacket. Tom was carried high up into the air, his legs dangling down as the raven flew across the sea.

Tom wriggled and shouted in the raven's beak, until the raven grew tired of holding him. It let go of Tom, who fell through the air until SPLASH – he fell into the sea! Just as Tom bobbed to the surface of the water, an enormous fish gobbled him up! As luck would have it, King Arthur's fishermen caught the fish in their net and took it back to the royal kitchen.

Tom surprised all the kitchen staff as he made his escape through the fish's open mouth. Tom's bravery impressed King Arthur, who invited him to have dinner at the royal table so that Tom could tell him of his adventures.

Tom Thumb told the King and Queen about many of his adventures. He told them of how his father drove a horse and cart back and forth from the fields to their cottage and how he wanted to try for himself:

"I asked my father, 'May I drive the horse home today?'

'How would you be able to hold the reins?' my father replied.

I thought for a moment, then said, 'I could stand in the horse's ear and whisper to him which way to go.'

'All right,' said my father. He lifted me up and put me in the horse's ear. The horse was happy to do as I instructed and soon we arrived home.

My mother came out to welcome us, but couldn't see me anywhere.

'Where's Tom?' she asked my father, alarmed.

'I'm up here, mother,' I called out, but she still couldn't see me. She never imagined I'd be inside the horse's ear.

'Mother, look up here. I'm in the horse's ear!' I shouted.

When my mother saw me, she laughed with joy, reached up and lifted me down.

'Father let me drive the horse,' I told her.

'Well done, both of you,' she said with a smile. Then we all went in for supper."

King Arthur enjoyed Tom's story and wanted to hear more, so Tom told him of the day when he was playing in the garden. A butterfly had picked him up and had flown away with him, eventually dropping him into a watering can. Tom had almost drowned, but managed to climb to safety up the spout! The King found Tom's stories so entertaining that he wanted to hear more and more.

When Tom's godmother, the queen of the fairies, heard the wonderful news that her godson had found favour with the King, she was very pleased. She asked her most skilful fairies to create a miniature chair for Tom so he could sit and dine on top of the noble table in comfort. The chair was made from silver birch and was beautifully gilded. When it was finished, it looked like a fairy throne.

King Arthur was so delighted by Tom that he presented the boy with a needle for a sword. Though not as magnificent as King Arthur's own sword, Excalibur, it was fine and sharp, and Tom wielded it as well as any of the knights at the castle.

A brown mouse was trained as Tom's horse, and he rode it fast and sure through the castle courtyards to the amusement of the King and Queen. King Arthur gave Tom a tunic embroidered with gold thread, trousers and boots fit for the adventurous lad and a hat with a feather plume that waved like a flag in the wind when the mouse picked up speed.

One day, a cat saw Tom Thumb's mouse,
With sharp claws bared it decided to pounce.
Tom used his sword to protect his friend,
And save the mouse from a sticky end.
The cat ran off, beaten in the fight.
Apart from some scratches,
The mouse and Tom were all right.

King Arthur gave Tom several silver coins from the castle treasury. Tom was to take them to his parents as a gift from the King to make their lives more comfortable. Tom put the coins in a purse made from a water bubble. It took him two days and two nights to carry them home on the back of the mouse.

Tom and the mouse travelled through the forest by day. As the light faded to twilight and then to darkness, Tom settled down next to the mouse. Together they sheltered from the cold night between gaps in the roots of trees, covering themselves with leaves when they were really chilly. Tom didn't get a lot of sleep because he kept a watchful eye out for any creatures that would do them harm. Apart from his needle sword, he kept a whip by his side made from a single strand of barley straw.

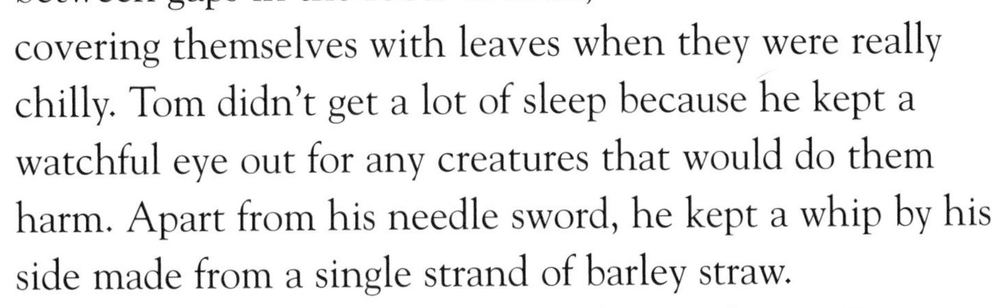

The journey was exhausting and quite daring. During their travels, Tom and the mouse came to the bank of a fast-flowing stream. With no bridge in sight, they decided to cross the stream on a raft.

Tom found a piece of wood that would make a good raft and a water reed he could use as a paddle. While the mouse clung to the raft as tightly as he could, Tom paddled hard to stop them both from being carried downstream by the strong current. Soon they were at the opposite bank where Tom helped the mouse scramble to safety.

There was also some trouble when Tom and the mouse stopped for a rest in a dark and shadowy part of the forest.

Tom was eating a blackberry when he heard a strange noise in the undergrowth. Fearing it was a wild animal, he told the mouse to hide. The mouse darted into a hole, while Tom threw leaves over the silver coins so that their shiny surfaces wouldn't attract attention.

With moments to spare, Tom dived headfirst into a ditch and crept into an empty snail shell. Tom sneaked a peak from beneath the shell and caught a glimpse of an enormous dog prowling past. The dog sniffed the air and turned his head in Tom's direction. Tom held his breath. He hoped that the dog hadn't been alerted to his hideout. Finally, the hound moved on, disappearing amongst the trees.

On the second day of their travels, a fierce wind began to blow. The wind was so strong that Tom was no longer able to cling to the back of the mouse. He climbed down and walked along in front, using all his strength just to stand up as leaves whipped past.

Despite all the dangers, the journey was very worthwhile. Tom's parents were very pleased with the gift from the King and were delighted to see their son.

Tom's mother had baked a cake to celebrate her son's visit, so Tom sat on a cushion beside the fire, munching on a slice of cake and sipping milk from a hazelnut shell.

"We're so proud of you, Tom," said his mother.

Tom's father nodded. "Yes, and please thank King Arthur for the generous gift of silver."

"I shall," said Tom, wiping crumbs from his tiny mouth. "His majesty is very good to me and often takes me with him when he is out riding. I hold on tightly to the horse's mane and if it rains, the King puts me in his waistcoat pocket so that I don't get soaked."

"That's very kind of him," said Tom's mother, pleased that the King was helping to look after her heroic little boy. She remembered how easily one large raindrop could drench Tom. He'd been out in the fields one day when it had started to rain and although Tom had been clever enough to use a flower to shield himself from the shower, a couple of drops had soaked him. By the time he got home, Tom looked as if he'd fallen in the river.

"What have you been up to this past while?" asked Tom's father. "Are you still getting into all sorts of mischief, even if it is no fault of your own?"

Tom sighed and smiled. "I am, father. My life is filled with lots of exciting adventures, but I wouldn't have it any other way." Tom went on to tell his parents about his encounter with a wolf who used its sly tricks to lure him so close that it could snap him up in its sharp-toothed jaws.

Tom's mother gasped in horror.

"The wolf didn't harm me," Tom explained. "I ran in circles around its feet so it couldn't catch me, and then Merlin used a magic spell to make it disappear."

"Phew!" sighed Tom's father. "You've had so many dangerous adventures. We are so glad that you are safe."

After visiting his parents, Tom rode his mouse back through the forest to King Arthur's castle. Just as they were walking across the main courtyard, a big spider spotted them with its beady eyes. It came scuttling towards them on its eight long, hairy legs and attacked poor Tom without mercy. People were watching from high turrets around the courtyard, knowing that they were too far away to save Tom Thumb from the vicious spider.

Tom drew his silver needle sword and fought as bravely as any of the King's knights… but the spider was too big for him. After many minutes of fierce fighting, it struck Tom down!

The people were shocked as they saw Tom's little body lying on the ground, his sword still clutched tightly in his hand.

"No!" they cried, "Tom's been killed by the spider!"

Then a miracle appeared to take place. Tom opened one eye and then the other. Beneath his tunic, he was wearing his favourite shirt woven by the fairies from a spider's web, and a spider's web is stronger than steel to someone as tiny as Tom. His special shirt had protected him from harm.

Tom Thumb lived to enjoy many new adventures with the King and Merlin the magician keeping a watchful eye on him. King Arthur honoured him for his bravery by knighting him Sir Thomas Thumb, a knight no bigger than his father's thumb.

THE END